Ivy of the Angel

and other stories

Also by Lena Kennedy

Maggie
Autumn Alley
Nelly Kelly
Lizzie
Lady Penelope
Susan
Lily, My Lovely
Down Our Street
The Dandelion Seed
Eve's Apples
The Inn on the Marsh
Owen Oliver
Kate of Clyve Shore
Queenie's Castle

About the author

Lena Kennedy lived all her life in the East End of London and wrote with great energy about the people and times she knew there. She was 67 before her first novel, *Maggie*, was accepted for publication. Since then her bestselling novels have shown her to be among the finest and best loved of contemporary novelists. Lena Kennedy died in 1986.

LENA KENNEDY

Ivy of the Angel and other stories

First published in Great Britain in 1993 by Little, Brown and Co.

This edition published in 2013 by Hodder & Stoughton
An Hachette UK company

1

A CIP catalogue record for this title is available from the British Library

Paperback ISBN 978 1 444 76747 6 ✓
Ebook ISBN 978 1 444 76748 3

Printed and bound by Clays Ltd, St Ives plc

Hodder & Stoughton policy is to use papers that are natural, renewable
and recyclable products and made from wood grown in sustainable
forests. The logging and manufacturing processes are expected to
conform to the environmental regulations of the country of origin.

Hodder & Stoughton Ltd
338 Euston Road
London NW1 3BH

www.hodder.co.uk

Ivy of the Angel

Old Ivy huddled in the dark doorway of the shop. Sniffing loudly, she shivered and pulled her ragged old coat closer about her bony shoulders. She peered miserably out into Oxford Street and the stream of passing traffic.

'It must be nearly nine o'clock,' she muttered. 'Surely they'll open soon.'

She was beginning to feel quite desperate. It had been very chilly in the park that night but, worst of all, the bottle in the paper carrier bag at her feet was empty.

Ivy felt quite dehydrated; her tongue was the texture of sandpaper and she felt in great need of a drink. The muscles of her haggard face twitched spasmodically as she rubbed her heavily veined hands together and then twisted the faded red woollen scarf around her neck for extra warmth.

Ivy was an alcoholic. In all her fifty years, she had been dried out many times but never for long. And she had been thrown out, raped, robbed and beaten senseless. Hospitals and institutions for the destitute were her homes and had been an integral part of her life for the last ten years. The social reformers had finally tired of Ivy's inability to pull herself together and had just abandoned her in despair.

Much of the time she slept in parks and doorways, even though the police frequently moved her on, calling her a bum. Ivy still had feelings about her situation. She knew that her life had reached its lowest ebb but she felt she had to keep going because although everything about her life was dreadful, she did not want to lose it, just in case there was something better somewhere for her one day. And besides, her favourite drink of cider with a dash of whisky could perk her up no end.

Ivy had tried prostitution for a while but that had failed because of the way she looked. No man wanted to pay money for the body of a drunken bum. Now Ivy had turned to shoplifting to get some money to keep herself going. She did not do it in the slick professional way from well-lighted store counters right under the nose of a store detective. No, she was not up to that; it would be too dangerous for her. Ivy's technique was to move slowly around the big stores looking out for someone's purse laid carelessly on the top of a shopping basket or a parcel put down for a second or two. With a quick swoop, Ivy would snatch up her booty, and scuttle away like a mouse with a piece of cheese. Then, later, she would barter her winnings for booze.

On this cold morning, the long wait for the shops to open seemed endless. Ivy felt colder, hungrier and thirstier than ever before.

At last there was movement inside the big store.

The lights had been turned on and the assistants were removing the dust sheets from the display counters. About time, thought Ivy. Now the day's business could begin.

With an extra shrug and a big sniff, Ivy emerged from her doorway and hobbled along on uncomfortable feet to the pedestrian crossing. The West End store was quickly coming to life. It had been gaily decorated for the festive season with hundreds of coloured balloons, tinsel and paperchains. To tempt the Christmas shoppers, the counters were full of exotic foods, dainty underwear and large displays of beads and brooches with the more expensive jewellery in glass cabinets alongside the watches and exquisite clocks.

It was to the jewellery department that Ivy now slowly edged her way, trying to mingle with the early shoppers. She did not know why but this department usually had more than its fair share of well-stuffed purses or carelessly dropped wallets.

But her luck was out that day. By noon, she still had not got anything. 'But not to worry,' she told herself optimistically. 'Something will turn up.' Looking around the room, her red-rimmed eyes settled on the sight of a young woman in an emerald green headscarf who seemed to be having an argument with the shop assistant.

The woman was shouting and waving her arms about. Ivy noted with interest the carrier bag that the woman had put down on the floor beside her. Suddenly, with an exasperated cry, the woman rushed off in the direction of the men's department.

Ivy moved swiftly. She went over to the bag on the floor, grasped the handle and trotted briskly into the empty lift. With an excited grin on her face, she pressed the button for the basement. From there she knew how she could escape through a back alley.

Ivy normally liked to examine her stolen booty well away from the shop she had taken it from, but she felt very curious about this lot. It was very heavy and wrapped in tissue paper. Her brain was not functioning very well – it never did until she had had a few drinks inside her – and she was very startled when the object in the paper suddenly started to make a loud whirring sound. She dropped the bag in fright. Images of last week's newspaper headlines flashed before her. It was a bomb. The IRA had given out a warning of a bombing campaign on the mainland in the run-up to Christmas. Ivy had read about it in the old newspaper she had used to cover herself at the weekend. She liked to keep up with the news, even if it was a little out of date.

Last week there had been a bomb in fact. A device had been left in a carrier bag in a big London store.

'Oh God,' Ivy exclaimed in panic, placing the bag in the farthest corner of the lift. The whirring sound was louder than ever. How much time did she have?

When the lift reached the basement floor, Ivy dashed out through the doors, only pausing to press the top floor button so that the lift would get as far away from her as possible before the bomb exploded. With a grimy hand she wiped the sweat from her brow. 'Fancy me nicking a bomb,' she muttered as she hobbled frantically towards the street door.

Then she noticed a young couple heading towards the lifts. With them they had a baby in a pushchair and another child no older than three who clutched a doll to her side.

Ivy hesitated and then stopped. In the depths of her mind she is transported back to a house in the Angel, Islington. In the house she can see two young children like those in front of her. They are laughing and larking about. A young woman, their mother, is with them. She is beautiful, with strong features and thick auburn hair. The mother is smiling at them but she has a worried expression in her eyes. Then a dark shape moves close to them. Her husband, with his coarse features and eyes already bloodshot from drinking. Bottles, half-empty glasses. Her husband, her drinking companion. Hangovers, fights, bruises. The house is a wreck, a slum. The children are screaming, first to stop the fights, then when the people from the social services come. Now the woman is screaming too. She does not look young anymore. Now she is haggard and old. Her face is lined, her hair dull and faded. The children are gone. The woman is crying, weeping. She drinks to make herself feel better. She has nothing left in her life. Staring at these little children now, Ivy knew what she had to do.

She yelled as loudly as she could: 'Get yer kids out!' Her voice had turned into a screech. 'There's a bomb in the lift.' With a loud wail, Ivy turned and ran in total panic into the street.

Ivy's message spread like wildfire throughout the store. People were rushing about in panic as they tried to get their children and themselves out of the shop. With no instructions from their superiors, the shop staff were not sure whether they should be helping the customers to leave or getting themselves out. They just did not know what to do and ran around in circles trying to find out.

Eventually someone dialled 999 and the police arrived quickly with blue lights flashing and sirens wailing as they began to evacuate the store. There had not been so much excitement in Oxford Street since the Blitz.

On the other side of the road Ivy stood and watched the panic-stricken people pouring out of the store. Although the police were urging everyone to move away and out of the danger area, people collected in groups to watch the excitement. 'Those Irish,' someone muttered. 'Something ought to be done about these things,' said another.

Ivy listened to their comments with some amusement. She could not understand why they were not just happy to be out of danger. Then she heard a loud voice say: 'That shop deserves to be blown up. I bought an alarm clock there last week and it kept whirring all night. When I took it back I couldn't find my receipt so they denied that I had bought it from there. I had a row with the assistant and when I went to get my husband to help, somebody stole the carrier bag with the clock in it.'

As Ivy heard these words, she began to feel very odd. Well, she had made a mistake, that was obvious, but what an amazing effect it had had. People were milling about all over the place. Sirens were blaring, police were shouting at the crowds through megaphones, telling them to move on. There was a tremendous sense of fear and excitement in the air.

Ivy needed a drink. She turned on her worn heels and hobbled off towards the supermarket where she might be able to nick a bottle of cider. As she walked along, she felt unusually jaunty. For the first time in many years she felt quite vital. Today she had not just been a passive down-and-out, one of the forgotten dregs of society. Today, she, Ivy, had made things happen, and that made her feel good.

Linda's Revenge

Even when I was a young child, my friends and family referred to me as a hardnut. Growing up as the only girl in a family of four tough boys, I learned from an early age to stand up for myself and not to rely on outside help of any kind. I carried this philosophy through my early life, and in those days I was proud to be considered so utterly independent.

I left my family home as soon as I could. It was not a happy place as my parents were always fighting, either with each other or my brothers and, later, me. For when I became a teenager, they turned their anxieties on to me and I realized that I had to escape before they made me a prisoner in the home.

It seems to me now that my life really began when I hitch-hiked to my first pop festival in Bath. It was the beginning of my involvement in the exciting world offered to the young in the late 1960s. It was an exciting grind for survival and to have one's voice heard. There were demonstrations against war, pop music for peace, and lots and lots of drug taking which turned us on and made us happy. And being fairly attractive, I always had a lot of boyfriends in tow.

In spite of the presence of all these boys, I was still

a virgin when I turned seventeen. This was not intentional; I think my famous temper certainly protected me. 'Don't get fresh with Linda,' my friends would warn a new admirer. 'Linda's got a punch like a prize-fighter.'

This wasn't the way I wanted things to be and at times I felt rather sad and lonely. Then I would begin to critize my appearance. I would stare down at my thick, sturdy legs and wish they were long and slim, and examine my boyish figure in the mirror and imagine how I would look if I were as thin as Twiggy, the girl we all modelled ourselves on in those days. I started dieting in a hopeless sort of way. I would starve myself, determined to achieve that controlled lean look needed for wearing tight jeans and skinny-rib sweaters, but I could never keep it up. After a month of misery and gnawing stomach pains, I would guzzle five cream cakes and quickly put on as much weight as I had lost, and more.

I was not very good at holding down jobs. I worked in cafés and pubs whenever I could, but I was not very punctual and the jobs never lasted for long. I lived in various digs, squatted in empty houses, as was the trend in those days, and after a year of living like this, I felt rather aimless. But I felt grown-up and glad to have left my family home when I did. I just was not sure where I was going.

Then I met Vivien and my life changed. Vivien was a sweet-natured girl a few years older than me. She was not good-looking but she had an attractive personality. She was warm and generous and had a motherly manner about her which appealed greatly to me. I had never felt very close to my own mother and I see now that Vivien answered a need in me at a crucial time.

We met when we were both queuing for a job. Vivien was standing in front of me and just from looking at her I knew I could not compete. She was smart, neat and clean, whereas I looked rather grubby and rumpled, having been rummaging around my squat at the last minute in an effort to find something presentable to wear. Nonetheless, she was not put off by my appearance and after the interviews she cheerfully offered me a cigarette and asked if I wanted to join her for coffee.

'I hope you're not too disappointed,' she said.

'I never wanted that stupid old job, anyway,' I said breezily.

We talked for a while and I was flattered that Vivien was so interested in me and my life. I told her proudly about the pop festivals and the squats and the hippie communities I liked to hang out in. But I was surprised by her response when I'd finished.

'Look, Linda,' she said kindly. 'I know this is not my business, and we don't even know each other, but you can't possibly go on living like this.'

I stared, almost glared at her. 'Oh, no?' I sneered. 'Suggest something better?'

Vivien did not react. Her voice was quiet and calm. 'Well,' she said, 'if you like you can share my digs. It's only one room and conveniences, and it's expensive. But it's big enough for two, and I was about to advertise for someone to share with me.'

I shook my head. 'That's impossible,' I said. 'I'm out of work and currently haven't a penny to call my own.'

Vivien shrugged. 'That's okay for the time being,' she said. 'I have enough to cover us for a week or so and I think we'll be okay until you get a job.'

I thought she was a mug to be offering me all this without knowing me at all. But that was her problem. 'Thanks,' I said. 'I'll come.'

Amazingly, that was the turning point for me after all these months of wasting time. Nothing happened immediately, but slowly some of Vivien's neatness and her niceness rubbed off on me. It must have done because, before long, I had landed a job in a department store and, in spite of my aggressive manner, held it down. I was not well paid but we were allowed a credit account for clothes. With Vivien's advice I learned how to purchase the kind of clothes that suited my sturdy frame. They were well fitting and tidy. Soon I did not even want to wear my multi-coloured, tie-dyed shirts and ragged jeans.

Vivien's digs were in central London. Before, I had been living in the suburbs so now I had to give up my suburban friends and build a new social life in town. On Saturdays Vivien and I would go to dance at the Drill Hall. On Sundays we would walk in the park.

It was on one of our Sunday promenades that Vivien bumped into Will, a boy from her home town. Will was out walking with a pal of his. Both wore army uniforms. Vivien and Will were clearly pleased to see each other. They looped arms and walked ahead of me and the other boy, laughing and chatting. The other boy and I trudged along behind. I'm sure that he was as embarrassed as I was by the display of affection in front of us. I was moody and sulky. I hated walking with this boy; all my hippie instincts made me hate anyone in uniform. He was a north country boy with ruddy cheeks and a slow drawl which intrigued me. He was very controlled and did not bother to compete when I tried to drag him into political arguments. And my provocative statements about law and order only made him smile. It seemed impossible to get a rise out of him, and I was surprised that I rather liked that.

We sat on the grass and waited for Viv and Will to walk about the lake.

'My name's Peter,' the boy said.

'Mine's Linda,' I growled.

'There's no need to be so aggressive,' he said lightly with a broad grin.

'And there's no need for you to be so condescending,' I snarled, lunging at him with my clenched fist.

Instantly, a strong arm came out and grabbed my neck, holding me in a vice-like grip. 'Want to play?' he jeered, and threw his weight on top of me.

Over and over we rolled in a very unseemly manner. I was determined to beat him but he was strong and well trained. I had not a hope. I gave up struggling and he sat on top of me, holding my arms on either side of my head as I lay on the cool grass. He hovered over me for a moment and then leaned back and pressed his hard lips on mine. It was an unforgettable first kiss.

'Come on, let's go, toughie,' said Peter, pulling me

up. I obeyed quietly, secretly thrilled to be taken over like this.

All that long hot month our romance blossomed. Peter was on leave for the whole time so he would meet me every evening outside the store when I finished work, and we would stroll home together. He told me about his family and upbringing and I, to my surprise, told him about mine. We shared all confidences and for the first time in my life I was hopelessly in love.

Vivien began to visit Will at weekends, so Peter would move in then. He shared my bed and I was only too happy to give up my virginity for him. We still fought but it was always friendly and very stimulating. We romped and wrestled and Peter even taught me a few army combat tricks. We shared a love for physical exercise.

I cooked for Peter and fussed over him in a way that I had never done to anyone in my life. I became house-proud and home-loving. I began to dream of marriage and even of having a baby. My personality had changed completely.

In the autumn Peter informed me that he was likely to be posted somewhere out of London. My heart beat wildly at the news as I was sure that he would now ask me to marry him so that I could join him.

But no proposal came. And I was astonished by what Peter did say: 'It's been great being with you, toughie, and I'll never forget you. I'll write to you, I promise.'

I stared at him in amazement. Surely this was a mistake. Surely I was interpreting his words in the wrong way, but it seemed to me that he was saying goodbye. Now I smiled and sidled up to him. 'Let me know where you're posted and I'll join you there.' I slipped my arms about his waist and hugged him.

He almost pushed me away. 'Now, don't hang on to me, Linda,' he said. 'It's been great fun being with you. Now just let it end how it began.'

I could tell from his expression that he meant what he said. I pulled away in sudden panic. 'But why?' I cried. 'Why are you saying this?'

Peter held my shoulders in both hands. 'Because I have a wife back home,' he said quietly. 'She is expecting another baby and I must get back soon.'

Now I did lose my temper. I went berserk. I kicked and scratched and tried to claw his eyes out. 'You bastard!' I yelled. 'You dirty bastard, how dare you use me like that!'

Peter backed away in alarm. He clearly had not expected me to react quite so violently. And he did not want to hang around to see much more of me. Grabbing his jacket, he hurriedly left.

I sat on the sofa for the rest of the afternoon weeping pitifully. He was the one and only person in the world I had ever loved. Now it was clear that he had never loved me, whatever he had said. I felt desperate – used and abused.

Later that evening I recovered a little but I felt very depressed and my head throbbed from all the weeping I had been doing. I realized that, in his haste, Peter had left behind some of his possessions – a razor, a packet of cigarettes, and a pocket book. I picked up these items and hugged them to me, imagining that I could smell his strong masculine scent. My heart ached and I felt that I could not live without Peter's love. But now, by losing my temper so violently, I had shown him my true colours. He would probably never come back again.

Thinking of the good times we had had, I turned over Peter's pocket book and then opened it. Inside were his army papers and a letter. Feeling guilty, but not enough to stop myself, I slipped it out and started to read. As I already guessed, it was from Peter's wife, whose name was Jenny. My eyes scanned the words but I did not take in their meaning because I was overwhelmed by a hot jealous fury. Screwing up the letter, I put it in my pocket. Then I wrapped up the other belongings and put them on the hall table.

The next day at work my bad temper and aggressive manner brought me a reprimand from my supervisor. But I could not snap out of my mood, however hard I tried. The day was a disaster and I was lucky not to have been fired on the spot. I was so glad when the day was over, but miserable as I stepped outside because there was no bright smiling face to greet me, no firm arm about my waist to escort me home.

When I got home, the hall table had nothing on it. Peter had obviously been in (probably with the help of Vivien) and taken his belongings. But there was no message for me. It was pathetic of me to have hoped that he might, I thought bitterly.

For the next few days I was desolate. Nothing Vivien

could say or do made me feel any better. 'Look, he's married, Linda,' she said over and over again. 'And he's obviously not going to leave his wife – she's having another baby, for God's sake. You must leave it at that.'

But I ignored my flatmate's sensible attitude. I fed my rage by reading that letter over and over again. Every time I did so, I could feel the emotion building up in my chest, and I would clench my fists so hard that my knuckles went white. The name Jenny became so imprinted in my brain that I found myself muttering it under my breath, as I did the address: Tithe Cottage, Rylstone, Yorks.

By Friday, my mind was made up. I drew my wages, put on my old shirt and jeans, packed my haversack and was off up the road. Hot violent hatred seethed inside me. I was going to find this Jenny and sort her out. If I could not have Peter, then neither would she . . . I would punish her for existing and Peter for deserting me.

To save time and expense, I took the coach for part of the way to Yorkshire and then hitched a ride for the rest. I was careful hitch-hiking and did well to choose a respectable middle-aged couple who, somewhat reluctantly, gave me a lift. I think they thought they would be saving my life by keeping me off the roadside. They dropped me off at a motorway café and I went in for coffee. I did not have much further to travel, so I could afford a bit of a break, I thought.

I sat down at a table with my cup of coffee. I was very preoccupied and did not notice anything about my surroundings.

'Anyone sitting here?' A cheerful voice startled me out of my reverie.

I did not look up but responded by shaking my head.

The person sat down. He was young and seemed anxious to engage me in conversation. Rattling the spoon in the sugar, he said, 'Excuse me,' in an unnecessarily loud voice. Even when he grinned at me over the rim of his tea cup, I tried to ignore him but it was hard not to notice his friendly smile and mop of jet-black hair. His strong rough hands indicated to me that he was a lorry driver.

'How did you get up here, then?' the man asked me directly.

I gazed at him in my most arrogant manner.

'I saw you outside Newmarket,' he said. 'I was going to pull up but saw you get in a car.'

'So what?' I growled in a hostile voice. 'I don't take lifts from lorry drivers.'

The man put down his cup with a clatter and stuck out his unshaven chin. 'Don't think all lorry drivers are the same, darling,' he said sarcastically. 'You're more likely to get raped by some toffee-nosed git in a posh car than by a hardworking lorry driver.'

'That's debatable,' I sneered.

My remark clearly annoyed him. He swallowed down the rest of his tea in one gulp and got up to go. 'I don't know where you're heading,' he said, 'but I do know that you're going to get into a lot of trouble with that attitude.'

I was not bothered by his comment. I was far too

concerned with my own affairs to care what he thought about me. I waited until I knew he had gone, then I made a few enquiries and found a bus to take me the rest of the way to Rylstone.

I arrived in Rylstone at about four o'clock in the afternoon. A black mist was beginning to rise over the hills and a strong wind blew me almost inside out. I went into a newsagent's and asked him where I could find Tithe Cottage. After much thought, the old shop-keeper told me that he thought it was way up the hill, about two miles out.

It was a long way to walk but I was still driven by my determination. I was cold and very weary but I trudged on up the hill, refusing to let myself stop for a moment. Dark clouds were gathering overhead and it looked as though the heavens would open at any moment.

There were not many cottages on that lonely road, just a few dotted here and there. Then, right at the top of the hill, I could see a small stone building standing back off the road. At the gate there stood a slim young woman, her golden hair flying out in the wind. She was holding a small boy by the hand and even from where I was I could see a firm round bulge in her belly. I knew immediately that this smiling Madonna was the woman I hated more than anything in the world. But oddly enough, my hatred did not feel very fierce at that moment, and I even realized that a smile was hovering on my lips in response to her welcoming look. Perhaps I was just too cold and tired to do anything else.

As I came up to the gate, the woman called out. 'Hello, we don't get many walkers at any time, let alone in this sort of weather.' Her voice was as soft and smooth as Peter's.

I stopped and breathed deeply to regain my composure.

'You're not going on over the hill at this time of day, are you?' Jenny looked quite concerned.

I nodded weakly.

'Oh, I shouldn't if I were you,' she said. 'It's mighty dangerous once the mist comes down.'

I rolled my haversack off my shoulder and dropped it on the ground. I stared glumly at Jenny. She did not look how I had hoped she would look. She was not ugly, she was pretty. She was not fat and dumpy, she was slim and lithe. And she was not old, she was young – not much older than me. I felt very depressed. She had everything going for her. What was I doing? I had got myself into a terrible mess.

I must have been looking very forlorn and lost, for Jenny opened the gate and held out a welcoming arm. 'Come in,' she said kindly. 'Come in and have a cup of tea. You look freezing.'

Slowly I followed Jenny and her little boy up the garden path. A large dog ran round the garden barking loudly to shrieks of excitement from the little boy. It was an enviable scene.

Inside the cottage Jenny led me to a cosy room with a low, beamed ceiling and a glowing fire. In the corner, the table had been laid for tea. It was a warm and comforting sight. Then I saw the crib in the other corner which contained two sleeping infants, fair-haired twins breathing rhythmically under their snow-white blanket.

I must have looked surprised or puzzled, because Jenny stepped over and whispered, 'Yes, they're all mine.' Then she went over to the table and began to pour two cups of tea from a shiny brown earthenware teapot. 'And I'm expecting another in the spring,' she added cheerfully, handing me the piping-hot cup. 'Help yourself to something to eat.'

I crouched by the warm fire sipping that hot tea and nibbling a homemade biscuit nervously. My ire, my reason for being there in that little cottage, had gone. I tried to summon it up again, I must hurt her, I told myself. She must suffer as I had . . .

But there was nothing there. That pent-up feeling had gone. I felt only remorse for myself, and, in fact, for the way this woman had been treated, too. The little boy played with a wooden train set at my feet; the young dog licked my hand enthusiastically. And Jenny was a constant and attentive hostess.

'It's very nice to have someone adult to talk to,' she said. 'I love my children dearly but you long for grown-up conversation after a few days alone. It's very lonely up here and my husband's away in the army.

'I was hoping that he would get leave during the summer so I was very disappointed when I heard that he'd been posted to Ireland. But he's got more leave now. In fact, he's coming home tomorrow for a couple of days,' she added with a confident smile.

I envied Jenny's composure. She was so sweet and unselfish. Not one word of complaint came from her lips. How would she react if I told her that Peter had spent that last lot of leave with me? I sat in silence feeling morose and confused. What was I going to do?

'Don't get me wrong by what I said about the children,' Jenny continued. 'They can be wonderful company and I enjoy being with them all the time. We both love the children. It's just . . .'

'But it's you who gets left having to care for them,' I said bitterly.

Jenny shrugged and smiled sweetly. 'Well, I guess that's just a mother's duty,' she said simply.

There was a faint stirring of rage as I went on. 'I'm not so sure,' I murmured. 'It's men who always get the best of both worlds. Especially,' I added darkly, 'if their work takes them away from home for long stretches at a time.'

Jenny laughed, stroking her son's soft dark hair with her hand. Her blue eyes gleamed fondly. 'I know what you're saying, but Pete's not like that, not my Pete. You see, we have been sweethearts since we were at school. He's never looked at anyone else, and neither have I.' She gazed at me with true innocence.

Now was the time to do it, I thought, trying to summon up the venom I needed to carry out my deed. But I could not. My tongue seemed to cling to the roof of my mouth. Not one vicious word could I utter.

I got to my feet and placed my tea cup on the table. 'Thank you for the tea,' I muttered. 'I'll be getting back down the road now.'

Jenny leaped up. 'Oh, but you don't have to go. Stay longer, if you wish,' she said. 'You're very welcome. In fact, you can stay the night, if you wish. My husband will be home tomorrow, and it would be nice to have some company anyway. I have enough food, I did a shop today.'

I swung my haversack over my shoulder. 'Oh, I wouldn't like to impose,' I said. 'Goodbye, and good luck with the new baby,' I called as I walked down the path and out into the road.

I plodded back into town, pushing against the strong wind. As I trudged along, the rage suddenly resurfaced, building up inside me like a great storm. I now realized that my rage had been misdirected before. I should not and could not hate Jenny, a woman of such pure goodness. It was that lying, cheating Casanova, Peter, who deserved every bit of my anger.

I stood beside the main road with my thumb out. The wind howled around me, whipping my hair across my face. I felt like howling with it. The rage was rampant inside me. Cars and lorries were roaring past. One lorry slowed down. I backed away but then remembered the words of that lorry driver in the motorway café.

'Going to London?' the driver called. He looked friendly enough and I reckoned that he would have been quite safe to travel with.

But then suddenly I shook my head at him and waved. 'I've changed my mind,' I shouted. 'I've decided I don't want a lift.'

The driver grunted, 'Suit yerself,' and slammed the cabin door before pulling out and trundling off down the road again.

As for me, I knew what to do.

I was puffing when I knocked on the door of that

cottage. The door opened and Jenny seemed delighted to see me. She looked radiant. The light from the room shone behind her thick hair like a halo. 'Have you changed your mind?' she asked. 'Do come in and get warm.'

'Thank you,' I said sweetly. 'I hope you don't mind but I hadn't realized how late it was. I would like to take you up on your offer of a bed for the night. It would be lovely to spend the evening with you and the children . . .'

Jenny was smiling with delight. 'Yes, and Pete will be home early in the morning, so you'll probably get a chance to meet him, too . . .'

I nodded slowly. 'Yes, I'd like that,' I said. 'It would be nice to see the whole happy family together . . .' And I knew that I did not care enough for her to stop myself.

The Lonely Road

I have often had a dream which seems to be a preview of the future that lies ahead for me. In the dream I am always walking along a hot, dry sandy road. A very bright sun burns down on my unprotected head and the ground is blistering underfoot. There is no other soul in sight and I feel terribly lonely walking down this long, winding road. Then suddenly, in the distance, I see a tiny figure coming towards me. I run to greet this person, who always wears pink, white and blue robes, of a flowing Biblical style. But I never get there, however much I hurry. The figure always remains in the far distance and I then awake, feeling frustrated and depressed. In a desperate attempt to interpret this dream, I have decided to write down the story of my recent life and the lonely road I have actually travelled.

I had a happy childhood, growing up in a respectable suburb. I was an only child and used to being alone for much of the time, brought up as I was by only my mother. She was a lively, bright little woman who travelled up to town each day to her job in an office, with which she supported us both. From as far back as I can remember, I washed and dressed myself and prepared my own breakfast before setting off on my own to school. And my mother would have left for work even before I had risen from my bed.

I was neither as quick nor as vivacious as my mother, whom I adored. In fact, I always felt myself to be rather unattractive, with skinny legs and thin black hair which I could never get under control. A friend of my mother once said that I had a kind of whimsical charm but I did not know what she meant then and I still don't.

I left school at sixteen and went up to the City to work in a typing pool. I would occasionally meet my mother for a sandwich at lunchtime, as she did not work far from me, but on the whole we lived more or less separate lives. For my gregarious mother had many friends from both work and outside and she loved to socialize with them whenever she could. Urged on by my mother, I did sometimes go to coffee bars and discos in an effort to ward off the loneliness that often gripped me, but in the absence of close friends such places only seem to accentuate any feelings of loneliness that exist. And on the rare occasion when I did have a date with a man, he was invariably dull, bespectacled and even more inhibited than I, so of course we bored each other stiff in no time. I had no social charm, no grace, and I certainly never expected anyone to find me attractive.

When I was about seventeen, at my mother's instigation, I took a holiday with two young girls from my office. It was at a holiday camp on the Yorkshire coast. We stayed in chalets and all day and all night there was entertainment of every kind on offer. If I had been a different sort of person, I might have enjoyed the wild fun. The place was full of young people who were determined to have a good time. They popped in and out of each other's chalets at all times of day and night, and consumed vast amounts of drink and pep pills to make the overall effect that much better. It was not my scene at all. I never drank alcohol – I hated the taste of the stuff – and I was far too frightened of the possible effects to take even the smallest pill. So I was always on the sidelines and considered by everyone else as a hopeless square. Generally, they all ignored me.

However much I hated that holiday camp – and I felt trapped there for the whole of the first week – it was the place where I met my Freddie. It happened at the swimming pool where I was sitting watching the antics of my companions as they larked about in the water with a gang of boys. A tall youth came over and sat down next to me, and I remember noticing his clear white skin, still dripping with water, and his rippling shoulder muscles. His sensual movements made me feel quite self-conscious as I sat there huddled in my black one-piece swimming costume.

He opened a small tin box and looked over at me. 'Want a roll-up?' he asked, holding out the tin.

'No, thanks,' I whispered, clearing my throat self-consciously. 'I don't smoke.'

I smiled timidly, glancing furtively at him as he leant back in the chair. He stretched his long legs and crossed them at the ankle in front of himself. I marvelled at that huge male body, with its strong physique, fair freckled skin and straight blond hair which stuck damply to his forehead above a clean profile. I was quite embarrassed to feel a thrill of excitement run through me as I peered at him through the screen of my long black fringe.

Suddenly a none-too-gentle hand grasped my hair and pulled it back from my face. The youth was leaning over and looking at me with a large grin. 'Stop peeping! Just take a good look, if you want to,' he said. He sat up and began to flex his muscles like a bodybuilder. He chuckled as he did this and had such an impish look on his handsome face that I burst out laughing. I think it was the first time in my life that I had ever reacted spontaneously. And I was smitten. From that moment I was head over heels in love with this good-looking youth from the East End of London.

Suddenly I had a boyfriend and I wasn't lonely anymore! For the rest of that week, I did everything with Freddie. We swam and sun-bathed during the day, and danced together in the evenings. We kissed and cuddled at every opportunity and every night he would get very drunk so I would take motherly care of him, and put him to bed, listening indulgently to his incoherent chatter and kissing him tenderly as if he were a baby.

At the end of the week, and by the end of the holiday, I had become pale and distraught at the idea of never seeing Freddie again. He did not say anything about continuing to see each other in London, and he seemed quite happy to say goodbye and go off with his pals after giving me a cheerful wave.

What makes one happy can also be the source of much unhappiness. During the weeks after my return from the holiday camp, I was utterly miserable. I could not eat and I lost weight. I mooned about and watched sentimental plays on the television, sniffing away the tears of my disappointment.

'Got a cold coming on?' asked my mother.

'No, just hay fever,' I snapped back at her.

My mother simply shrugged and went back to doing the office accounts, which she often did at home to earn extra cash. I longed to dash over to her, put my head in her lap and pour out my heart. But as always I was held back from saying what I felt by some built-in restraint I think I was born with. There seemed to be a great barrier between us and all I could do was hold on to my lonely memories. And I was afraid that they would be the only happy memories I would ever have.

I was back at work and feeling as isolated as ever. During the lunch break I would take my sandwiches and sit in the square to watch the busy crowds passing by. My thoughts were always on Freddie, my boyfriend for a week. At first I felt hopeless about the situation, but then one day, for no obvious reason, I suddenly felt strong and positive. Instead of sitting here waiting for something to happen, I thought, I should be doing something myself. After all, I reasoned, Freddie has enjoyed himself with me, so it was perfectly possible – certainly not a crazy idea – that he was now looking for me. In fact, it was possible that he was in one of these thronging crowds, searching for me at this very moment.

All sorts of ideas flew around my head. Suddenly I knew what I had to do. I would find Freddie myself. He lived in London, so it should not be too difficult, I reasoned.

I started off by making enquiries at my office. There

were plenty of cockney girls working at the typing pool and I knew that the East End was a tight-knit community. The chances were that one of the girls would know my Freddie. All I had to do was not be afraid of admitting my interest in this young man.

It worked. It was Doris, with the heavily lacquered, peroxide hair and bright red lips who came up with the information I wanted. 'I know blond Freddie,' she said. 'Lives in the next block, he does. All that gang of boys does. A rough lot of tearaways, they are. Me muvver won't let me mix wiv them.'

That last remark should have been a warning to me, I suppose, but I was so excited by this new information that I did not stop to analyse Doris's words. And, like a private eye, I set about finding my Freddie.

Every evening I left the office and got the tube to the East End. There I emerged to wander around the gloomy district, focusing mainly on a huge block of flats where I was now sure Freddie lived. But where, exactly? It was a high tower and, every time I looked up, it seemed that a myriad of windows and balconies stared soberly down at me. What if my search were to prove fruitless? I thought anxiously.

But I struck lucky at the end of my first week of hanging around like this. I was sitting in a dingy café having a cup of tea when I noticed an untidy youth playing on a very noisy one-armed bandit. As I looked at him, he stared back at me, rather insolently, I thought.

'Don't I know you?' he said. He certainly did not suffer from shyness. 'Wasn't you on that holiday camp?'

As he spoke I recognized him as one of Freddie's pals

at the camp. I grinned at him with a tremendous sense of relief. I was that much closer to seeing my Freddie.

Within ten minutes I was knocking timidly on a red painted door with frosted-glass panels. There was no reply. I stood hesitantly on the doormat and was wondering whether to drop a note through the letter box, when a small dark woman in carpet slippers came puffing along the balcony carrying several heavy bags of shopping.

The woman peered at me suspiciously. 'Yer want me?' she asked. She looked very slovenly.

'No,' I called back. 'I was looking for Freddie.' I faltered a little at the thought that this was Freddie's mum. She did not look like him at all.

'Freddie ain't in,' she said flatly, putting down a shopping bag and reaching into her pocket for the door key. 'And 'e never is in until it's late,' she added.

I tried to look casual. 'Would you please tell him that Lorna called?' I asked. 'And give him my address?'

The woman stared at me and grunted. 'Well, I suppose I can,' she said, 'But I don't know as he's going to like it. Freddie ain't usually one for the gels. Likes the company of 'is mates, 'e does.'

I scribbled down my name and address on an envelope and handed it to her. 'Thank you very much,' I whispered, my courage rapidly draining from me.

The woman took the envelope quickly and turned her back on me rather deliberately as she put the key in the door. I felt that she was anxious to get rid of me and I suddenly felt depressed and gloomy.

She glanced at me as she opened the door. Seeing

my unhappy expression, she seemed to have a change of heart. 'Come Sunday, love,' she said, a sweet smile appearing on her lined face. 'You'll catch Freddie on Sunday, 'cos 'e always stays in bed nearly all day then.' With that, she quickly bustled indoors and closed her front door.

I was breathless with happiness. I had done it! I had taken action and found my Freddie! And I had done it all on my own . . . I felt heady with elation.

On Sunday I began to get ready to set off for the East End soon after lunch.

'Going to the pictures, Lorna?' asked my mother.

'Yes,' I lied. 'There's a good film on in town.' I hated being untruthful to her but I was still incapable of confiding in her. I had to keep my secret clutched to my chest.

'Well, don't be home late,' my mother called as she settled on the settee for a snooze. Sunday afternoon was the only time in the week that she kept to herself. I crept out of the house with my old coat over my best outfit and set off again for the East End.

I found the tower block without difficulty this time, and before long I was knocking again at the red door. After a few minutes it was opened by Freddie's mother. She was looking very tousled and somewhat surprised to see me.

'I've . . . I've come to see Freddie,' I stammered, trying to sound as polite as possible.

The woman rolled her eyes. 'Oh, dear,' she muttered, glancing backwards to indicate the blue-carpeted corridor behind her. 'He ain't up, dear.' she said. 'And he ain't been in bed very long, either.'

I felt desperate. My lips trembled and tears crept into my eyes. My sense of bravado was wearing off fast. 'I'll wait, if necessary,' I whispered. 'But I simply must talk to him.'

The woman looked me up and down with a quizzical expression on her face. The suddenly she saw what it was all about. Her face softened and she reached out to touch my arm. 'Come in, love,' she said with a knowing smile. 'Don't get upset.'

Freddie's home seemed to be furnished with every modern convenience I had ever seen or heard of. The small flat was packed with televisions, stereos, toasters, kettles; there was not an inch of spare space anywhere. It was also rather dirty and untidy. Cups half-filled with cold tea sat on the mantelshelf, and on the glass coffee table were several grubby plates containing half-eaten sandwiches which now looked stale and curled at the edges.

'Sorry abaht the mess, love,' Freddie's mother apologized. 'Freddie and his mates had an early breakfast.' She swept up the plates and started tidying up busily. I thought she looked like a little cock sparrow as she hopped back and forth from the sitting room to the kitchen.

I sat and waited, sipping the hot tea Freddie's mum handed me. 'My name's Maureen, love,' she said. 'You can call me that if you like.'

The hours passed and still Freddie did not emerge from his warm bed. At one point Maureen went down the corridor to see if he was getting up and a lot of shouting and screaming went on. It scared me rather, and I almost ran away that minute. But I stayed, stuck like the Rock of Gibraltar in the middle of the smart new settee.

I found it quite difficult to make conversation with Maureen who was clearly rather harassed. I think she found the situation just as hard and so her solution was simply to ply me with more tea and sticky cakes. At one point she did ask me, rather abruptly and in a cracked, hoarse voice, 'You ain't in no trouble, are you, love?' She had a worried look on her round face.

I was so green I had no idea at all what she was implying. I smiled at her in a somewhat apologetic manner and did not say anything. Little did I realize that she took the vagueness of my response to mean that I was in trouble. How could I have known when I did not even know what she meant? But certainly her manner towards me suddenly changed, and from then on she sat reading the Sunday paper in what seemed like solemn gloom with scarcely a word in my direction.

The door to the sitting room was shut and so I did not hear noises to indicate that Freddie was up and about until the front door suddenly slammed. By now it was seven o'clock in the evening. Maureen and I both turned to the window to see Freddie beating a hasty retreat down the balcony, long blond hair and shirt tails flying.

The sight was too much for me. Now the bottled-up tears began to flow.

Maureen looked embarrassed. 'Never mind, love,' she said. 'Have some coffee.' As she got up to bustle back to the kitchen, she was muttering under her breath, 'The little so-and-so . . .' And the string of swear words that followed expressed her disapproval of her son's behaviour. I was only glad that it was not directed at me. 'Freddie will be back when the pubs shut,' Maureen said when she brought in a tray of coffee and fresh sandwiches. 'We'll catch him then.'

I marvel now at how gauche I was as a teenager. It never occurred to me to go home then. I just sat in deep depression on the sofa in that quiet sitting room with the brass carriage clock ticking merrily on the mantelpiece, awaiting my fate.

At two minutes after ten o'clock, Freddie returned. We heard him approaching, whistling cheerfully as he walked down the balcony. The front door opened and closed and then he stepped into the sitting room, his mouth open to greet his mum. When he saw me, he shut his mouth and backed away in what looked like sheer terror. I don't know who was more frightened, him or me.

Quick as lightning, Maureen shut the door and leant against it. 'You bloody sod!' she yelled. 'This gel's been waiting for you all day.'

Freddie shot me an embarrassed glare. 'Come on, then,' he growled, 'I'll take you to the station.'

Suddenly everything seemed to be all right again. As I walked beside my tall Freddie, all I felt was a burning sense of pride inside me. Even Freddie's harsh words did not dent it. 'Look here, kid,' he growled as we walked down the high street, 'don't come down here running after me no more. I'm not your type and we live in completely different worlds.'

'I don't agree, Freddie,' I replied primly, astonished by my own confidence. 'I love you.'

There, the words were out. I stared up at his handsome face with love in my eyes.

Freddie noticeably flinched and sighed. 'Look here,' he said again, 'that was different. It was just a bit of fun. I don't want no regular bird, and besides, I ain't no good. I'm always getting into trouble.'

The words went in one ear and came out the other for all I heard. We had reached the long, deserted alley that led to the station. I stopped, leaned against the wall and looked up pleadingly at him. 'Oh, Freddie,' I cried, 'please don't send me away.' In a fit of boldness, I threw my arms around his neck and pressed my body close to his.

To my relief and joy, Freddie responded. He pulled me to him and squeezed me tight. 'You're a funny little bird,' he murmured, nuzzling my hair before moving his firm lips down my neck towards my mouth.

We stood for a long time in that alley. Freddie's kisses tasted like wine, though it was probably only the brown ale he had been drinking.

I was very determined. Freddie was mine now, and he seemed to go along with this. He held me tight and repeatedly said, 'Funny little bird, ain't yer?'

I could not have been happier. On that last train home, my heart sang like a real bird. I had won my battle, Freddie was mine. It is very hard now to believe that I was so foolish, but I was seventeen years old and all that I cared about was that I had won my man.

And so began our heavy courtship. Freddie and I met every night after work. I was drawn into his world and became more and more involved with him, sitting in a dirty old pub night after night, sipping my lemonade while Freddie played darts with his pals, downing pints by the dozen, it seemed. When it was time, he would stagger with me towards the station and we would make love in the dark alley before I got on the train home.

On Saturday nights we went to his house, while his mum was at bingo. We would make love and then end the evening in the same old dreary pub with Freddie as drunk as a newt. But did I ever complain? Did I ever murmur one word of protest at this utter waste of time? Of course not. I was too happy with the good things to risk complaining about the bad, and I went along with it with good humour. What a silly little nit I was, filled up to the brim with notions of romantic love.

Freddie did not have a regular job. He said it would be too boring. Instead, he often did casual work for a local coal merchant. It did not take long for me to realize that this work merely subsidised the little fiddles Freddie was involved with. It did not bother me, just as it did not bother me that most of my hard-earned spending money went on buying him and his mates drinks when he had run out, or that he could not be bothered to change out of his working clothes in the evening so that I would come home with my own clothes covered with coal dust.

My mother began to get quite anxious about the state of my clothing without knowing the true reason for it. When she did the washing, she would always start muttering, 'Shocking black marks. Don't they ever have your offices cleaned? It's a disgrace and not the right way to treat the work force.'

'Well, they've got the decorators in,' I lied.

'Must be the cheapest firm they could find,' my mother grunted.

Then one Saturday afternoon my world caved in around me. I had been through the market and picked up a pretty bunch of flowers for Maureen and some beef sandwiches for our supper. I was in a good mood and for once did not even wrinkle up my nose at the smell of urine in the box-like lift that chugged up to Freddie's floor. Maureen opened the red door and I could see immediately that she had been crying. Her eyes were red and bloodshot and a cigarette hung miserably out of the corner of her mouth.

'He's not here, love,' she snivelled. 'He's gorn away. Didn't you know?'

I stared at her blankly. 'What do you mean?' I felt a horrible chill creep through my body and I knew that something was very serious. 'Gone away?'

Maureen nodded miserably. 'Yes, love. And 'e got six months, which 'e thought 'e would.' She wiped away a tear with the back of her rough hand.

Slowly it dawned on me what she was talking about. 'Do you mean he's been arrested, or something?'

Maureen nodded. 'Yes, love, and more than that,' replied Maureen. 'Freddie's in the nick. He was out on bail. Didn't he tell you?'

I shook my head silently. I felt quite hopeless. The lump in my throat prevented me from saying anything – not that I knew what to say.

Maureen ushered me inside the flat, 'Well, we have to look on the bright side, I suppose,' she said. 'The good thing is that he'll only do four months. They always get remission.'

She jabbered on, using words that seemed like those from a foreign language and I could not take any of them in. I wearily handed her the flowers I had bought. 'Am I allowed to write to him?' I asked.

Maureen nodded. 'Of course you are,' she said. 'Here's the address.' She handed me a crumpled piece of paper, which I slipped into my pocket. Then slowly and dreamily I left, going down in the lift and on out into the high street as if in a trance. There was a lot of noise and traffic which normally I would find annoying, but I did not notice any of it. On the way home, I sat in the corner of the train carriage weeping my eyes out, not caring that all the other passengers were staring at me curiously.

My mother looked very concerned when I came home so early and went to my room without a word, but she made no comment.

From then on, I wrote many letters to Freddie, long unashamed love letters which I stamped and posted religiously before waiting in vain for a reply. It was an agonizing time. Then one morning, on the mat lay a strange blue envelope clearly marked: FROM HER MAJESTY'S PRISON. My mother picked it up before I could get there and was staring at it in wonder.

'That's for me,' I snapped and grabbed the letter from her. I fled to my room to open it and was disappointed to see that it was just a brusque note from

Freddie thanking me for writing to him and asking me to visit him. Well, after all this waiting, it was better than nothing. I held the note tight to my breast and almost danced down the stairs.

My mother was standing at the bottom of the stairs with a stern look on her face. I had not seen such an expression from her since I was a child and in need of telling off.

'Who's writing to you from prison?' she demanded.

'It's none of your business,' I replied rudely.

'That is where you are wrong, young lady,' my mother replied, whipping the letter from my grasp.

I screamed at her and tried to snatch back the letter. But my mother slapped me in the face. I sank down on the stairs weeping loudly as my mother put on her spectacles and read the note. 'So this is from the boyfriend you've been so secretive about,' said my mother coldly.

I nodded miserably. 'Yes, Mother,' I wailed, 'and I love him. This is breaking my heart.' I was sure that she would sympathize with my plight. I was wrong.

'Lorna,' she said, kindly but firmly, 'you must give this young man up. Write him a nice letter and tell him it's all off. Blame me, if you like, tell him that I did not approve . . .'

She had worked it out like that, in a flash. It was all so cut and dried, and the calmness of her tone infuriated me. I snatched back the note which she had neatly folded and began to sob hysterically. 'I won't do any of that,' I yelled. 'I won't, I won't!'

My mother did not flinch. 'Now, stop being so foolish, Lorna,' she said. 'You're making me late for work.

And you should get off to work too, or you'll be in trouble.' She adjusted her wrist watch by the hall clock, slipped on her jacket and picked up her case. Pecking me on the cheek, she opened the front door and left.

For a long time after my mother had gone. I sat on the stairs immersed in self-pity. I did not go to work that day. I called in sick and stayed in my room writing passionate love letters to my Freddie. All reason had left me. I told him that I would come to see him the following week.

The atmosphere between my mother and me was cold and tense. We rarely spoke to each other and she kept glancing at me with a worried expression on her face. She knew that I was determined to defy her. Halfway through the week, she pleaded with me. 'Don't go to visit that boy, Lorna,' she begged. 'Be sensible. It will only hurt you more if you pursue him. Just make the break while he is away. It will be easier for you that way.'

I ignored her, refusing to look up from the newspaper I was reading.

'Darling,' she choked with genuine emotion, 'don't ruin your life, as I have done. Just think before you allow yourself to fall into an existence that you know nothing of . . .'

I was touched by her pleas but fought hard not to respond. I gritted my teeth and looked coldly at her, but how I longed to run and cuddle that pretty blonde head against my breast and comfort her. I knew what she was referring to. I knew how hard she had struggled to forget my father's incorrigible infidelity, and be like two parents to me. But I felt I had to win this. I loved Freddie and I would obstinately hang on to him in whatever way I could.

'Just mind your own business!' I yelled at her.

My poor mother burst into tears and went upstairs to her lonely bed.

My first visit to Freddie in prison was not a great success. I was horrified and awed by the imposing gateway, the high walls, and the long, dingy corridors. When I first arrived at the big gate, a smaller door inside the main door opened and a prison officer in blue uniform and a peaked cap scrutinized me and asked me my business. I had a bizarre desire to laugh I was so nervous. I was taken inside and shown the place where visitors could meet the prisoners. Soon I was sitting opposite Freddie who sat behind a little window of glass and wire. He looked very embarrassed and was certainly uncommunicative. Oh, how I longed to kiss and hug him but the chicken-wire made that impossible.

After that first visit, I got used to the scene inside the prison, and Freddie loosened up. Before long, we could laugh and make jokes again, and look forward to the future and Freddie's release.

After a few weeks, Freddie was transferred to an open prison. This was much nicer because we were allowed to sit together and touch and share a cigarette. All his plans and enthusiasm for getting out gave me a lift, and I was amused by all the tricks he taught me to get around the prison rules. He showed me, for instance, how to pass him a pound note without being detected. I had to fold it into a tiny shape and put it between my lips for the farewell kiss. It was fun having such little secrets and I became very adept at these dodges. Freddie was impressed by my skill, and every visit brought us closer.

At last Freddie's sentence was over. After four months, as Maureen had predicted, Freddie was released. I was on the train platform to welcome him back to freedom when he arrived in London. Over the next few weeks I was introduced to more of life's experiences – like coming-out parties that went on all night, extreme drunkenness and four-letter words I had never heard before.

I was ecstatically happy to have Freddie back and to be part of his world again. My mother and I hardly ever spoke to one another now. She always looked rather sad and worked even harder than ever. But I was too selfish to worry about her state of mind.

I felt very self-contained, and I had to be. Freddie had made lots of new friends and acquaintances in prison and these were the people he hung out with now. I had very few friends among them. These people regarded me as toffee-nosed and therefore not entirely trustworthy. Ironically, the girls in the office, informed of my attachment to Freddie by gossipy Doris, regarded me as not-quite-nice. To my mother I was a crazy little fool who would soon come a cropper.

But I did not care what any of these people thought just so long as I had a happy, laughing Freddie beside me to love and bully me. I pestered him continually to marry me.

I cannot deny that I was a selfish little fool, eaten up

by my own egotism. All I cared about was satisfying my intense need to be loved. I had no thought for my own loving mother or for a boy who wanted to remain free. No, I was determined to put a yoke around the neck of a youth who had been deprived from birth and hemmed in by circumstance. Weighing up the situation now with hindsight, I cannot think of one thing to my credit.

In an effort to ease matters at home, I did try to introduce Freddie to my mother. Of course it was a complete disaster. Freddie deliberately behaved badly – authority of any sort brought out the worst in him, and to him any parent was an authority. And my mother, understandably, decided that he was an ill-mannered oaf.

My next move was perhaps the silliest one I have ever made. Freddie had changed since he had come home. He was much more assertive and sexually aware. He knew exactly what he wanted and how to obtain it. He had a delivery job driving a small van and we often made love in the back of it, in all sorts of places. We were careless about contraception. Freddie assured me that absolutely nothing could happen, and I trusted him.

Of course the inevitable happened. In no time I had become pregnant. I became very queasy in the mornings and exhausted in the evenings. My mother recognized the signs immediately. I shall not dwell on the scenes that followed but suffice it to say that her I-told-you-so attitude infuriated me. The last tenuous link of love was almost severed in that last disgusting swearing match I had with my lovely mother.

I was comforted by the fact that Freddie was unperturbed by the latest development. 'Well, we'd better get hitched,' he muttered in a matter-of-fact manner.

'But where will we live?' I asked.

'Better bunk in with me mum, I suppose,' replied Freddie.

The very thought of living in that grubby, untidy flat with his mother appalled me, and I walked the streets for days in an effort to find a flat for us to make our own home. Of course, this was an impossible hope in overcrowded London for two young people with hardly a penny to their name. In order to earn more money, I switched from my job to temping. It did pay better but it was much harder work and extremely lonely.

Freddie seemed very unconcerned about the situation and he did little to find himself a well-paid job. He still just loved to spend time with his pals. Every evening I would return home from work to an empty house, as my mother had taken to avoiding me. I would change and then set out for the East End to track Freddie down in whatever pub he was hanging out in with his pals.

We finally got married, or hitched, as Freddie always referred to it. By that time I was six months pregnant and unable to hide the bump under my loose-fitting smock. We went to the registry office at the town hall. I can still see my mother's sad white face even now. She was dressed in a neat fur coat and a smart hat. Beside her stood Freddie's mum, Maureen, in a cheap, brightly coloured dress and a flowery hat which made her shrewish features look positively comical.

Afterwards there was a party at Maureen's flat. My mother did not come. There a huge crowd of strange faces wished me luck and made the crudest jokes. And Freddie did not stop drinking so that he became so drunk he was unconscious for the whole of the next day.

I had given up trying to find our own place and we moved into Maureen's flat. It was dire. The soul-destroying loneliness of those housing estates is inconceivable to someone who has never experienced it. I discovered this within the first few weeks of married life. It was as hard for Maureen as it was for me, I think. Anyway, she quickly got herself a job and spent her spare time with another married son. Freddie was equally elusive. Marriage had not affected his attitude to home life one bit. He dashed out of bed late for work every morning and would not even have time for a cup of tea. Then in the evenings, he would arrive home very late, after the pubs had closed, and fall into bed befuddled with drink.

I was not very happy. I would spend many hours looking over that balcony down into the maze of narrow streets below. Pregnancy had made me more fearful and I had become afraid to enter that smelly, claustrophobic little lift in case I got molested. Those were lonely days for me, with no company except the baby kicking inside me.

Three weeks before the baby was due, Freddie suddenly dashed home looking very excited. 'Come on!' he yelled. 'We're moving, we've got a flat.' Breathless with excitement, we hurriedly packed our few belongings and Freddie drove me to our new home.

Our flat was not very far away at all, just nearer the river, in dockland, in fact. It was in an ancient block of flats, and was not high up, being on the fourth floor, but we had to walk up eight flights of filthy stone steps to reach our new abode. On every landing there was a lavatory with a door hanging open and emitting a disgusting stench. Children scampered about everywhere, and in almost every doorway we passed stood a frowsy, unwashed woman scrutinizing the newcomers.

I stumbled up the steps puffing hard as I carried a suitcase, while Freddie leaped up them two at a time with perfect ease in spite of carrying an extremely heavy case. I smiled at the sight of my man, so fit and agile.

With a proud grin on his face, Freddie showed me into our flat, our home, if you could call it that. I stared in absolute horror at the dirty walls and the obscene graffiti scribbled all over them. Tears of despair pricked my eyes as I looked around the grubby drab rooms. The furniture was old and battered, much of the upholstery torn and stained. The place looked as if it had not been cleaned for years.

'Not such a bad pad,' said Freddie cheerfully. 'Me mate got nicked. He'll be away for a few years and his missus has hopped it. She gave me the key. It's ours for a long time, me darling.'

I stared at him in disbelief. Did he really feel proud to have got us these ghastly two rooms plus kitchen? I did not say a word but my thoughts must have been written all over my face as I stared disdainfully around the place.

'Now, don't turn your nose up,' Freddie said. 'You should think yourself lucky,' he added caustically. Going to the door, he turned and said, 'You unpack and clean up the place and I'll go and get some fish 'n' chips.' With that, he was gone, and I knew he would be gone for hours.

Slowly and methodically I began to clean up the place. Knowing that I should be pleased to have a roof over our heads that was ours, I set about making the place into a home.

It was hard work. The filthy lino, unwashed crockery and rickety bed really sickened me. As I emptied the dirty water down the communal sink on the landing, little children watched me with large dark eyes. From the doorway down the hall, a long-legged black woman called out, 'Hello, honey, just moved in, have you?'

She too was obviously pregnant but I did not feel like talking to her. Ignoring her, I pushed past the children and shut our door with a slam. What a nasty little bitch I was! That friendly smile of welcome was always missing in my life in those days, for whenever one appeared I would turn away.

With the sheer drive of determination I did manage to turn that dreary slum into a habitable home. We had very little money, of course, because, in addition to the usual reasons, Freddie had also paid a generous advance to the woman who had wished so hurriedly to vacate the flat. Freddie still had no regular income and preferred to do casual work, so there were some weeks when we were terribly poor. And we had to live like that, from week to week.

But Freddie's charm and personality won through as usual. He got on well with our neighbours, black and white. One of them lent him tools, another gave him a plant. He still came home drunk every evening, and when he was in the money he threw pennies on the landings for the children to scramble for and played cards with their fathers at the weekends. Yes, Freddie was well in with the other inhabitants of our block but I remained cold and aloof. I had no desire to mix with anyone.

After a while, my mother called on me. Arriving in a taxi, she came to my front door and burst into tears when she saw me.

I suppose I must have been a bit of a shock to her. My hair was lank and untidy, and instead of a proper maternity frock, I just wore an old dress which was bursting at the sides. The lack of facilities made it difficult to be fussy about one's appearance and I suppose I had just stopped bothering.

I was pleased to see my mother, and I petted and fussed her and tried to reassure her that everything was all right. I did not admit to any unhappiness at my plight, I just pretended to be wonderfully content. I showed her all the work I had been doing, the walls I had painted, the knitting I had done for the baby. But she was not fooled. Her eyes were tearful when she left and she shoved a five-pound note into my hand, for the baby, she said. I was grateful for that; there was not a bean in my purse.

So I lived like this for what seemed weeks while I waited for the baby. I painted anything and everything that would take paint – walls, doors, chairs, wardrobes, floors. I felt as if paint would be the only thing that could cheer up our gloomy abode. Sometimes I was sick with hunger, sometimes faint from fright when the two other families on our landing indulged in a big fight, as they were wont to do. It was a grim existence.

One evening, I was holding up my arm trying to paint the top of a door when my labour pains began. I began to sweat and shiver at the same time. I got down off the chair I had been standing on, picked up my little case which I had already packed, and set off slowly down those smelly stone steps. It was only nine o'clock. Freddie would not arrive home before midnight and there was no way I knew of to contact him.

My hand slithered along the rough iron rail. I can remember those moments so vividly. I was terrified that my baby would bounce out of me and fall down those steep stone steps. How ignorant I was! I still had many hours of labour to go but I could be excused because I was almost insane with fright.

I went to the telephone box and dialled the ambulance. Then I waited all alone in the cold, blinding rain, groaning at every contraction, until the ambulance arrived.

The next morning my baby son was born in the London Hospital. I lay in bed exhausted, trying to erase those anxious moments from my memory.

Freddie arrived in the afternoon. He had already been celebrating by the look and smell of him. He stood by the baby's crib, laughing and joking with one and all, extolling the merits of his baby son. He was the proud father all right.

My mother did not come to the hospital but, on my return home a few days later, I discovered the reason why. There was a card from her saying that she had gone on holiday for a few weeks, staying with a friend who had a villa in Spain. I felt very hurt that she should go away at such a crucial moment in my life but then I knew that I had hurt her badly over the past two years, too.

But Freddie's joy at being the father of a son knew no bounds and his celebrations went on for days. One night he got paralytically drunk and crashed the van, and was arrested for drunken driving. He was banned from driving, despite his pleas that he would lose his livelihood if disqualified. His insolent behaviour in court probably did not impress the magistrate in the right way.

So now our means of subsistence had disappeared along with the van. Now we had to live on social security, which, to me at least, was a terrible social stigma.

Freddie did not care. 'Don't be so soft,' he scoffed. 'It's only what every working-class family is entitled to.'

I shook my head. 'I don't like living on charity,' I protested. 'I'm not scounging off the welfare state.'

Freddie sniffed scornfully. 'It's what we all pay for,' he said aggressively. 'And I'd only be a bloody fool trying to keep you on twenty quid, labourer's wages.'

His attitude made me very uncomfortable but I was in no position to argue.

The days after our son was born just drifted by in

that blurred fog that follows birth. I was with the baby all the time, trapped in that endless routine of feeding, sleeping, nappy changing and laundry. And, after all, I began to lose some of that false pride as conditions eased off. I stopped worrying about living on the social security and just did it, plus the few odd pounds that Freddie provided from the occasional job here and there.

In fact, Freddie made no attempt to get a proper job, even now. He was out all day with his mates, and at one time told me that he had a little fiddle going. He didn't tell me what it was or give me any other details, but occasionally he would return home loaded with presents. I soon forgot about the fiddle and accepted his word that he had earned the extra cash doing a job for a bloke. Whenever he had money, Freddie would spend it lavishly on expensive toys for Kevin, our boy, or even flowers for me. I shall never forget that big bunch of red roses he bought me in the middle of winter. They must have cost a fortune and they looked so exquisite, so pathetically beautiful standing in the old jam jar on the mantelpiece amid those drab surroundings.

So I was reasonably happy during that time. Once the baby was tucked up in his cot, I would sit and wait, looking forward to Freddie's breezy, bright company later that evening.

One day in the spring I received another letter from my mother. In it she announced that she had met a wonderful man out in Spain and that she intended to stay out there for the immediate future. I was pleased for my mother. She had been on her own for so many years, but I also felt horribly deserted. But I know that she just could not bear to be around and see the conditions in which I lived. She was very upset by the road I had chosen to take in life and did not want to witness it. However, she did suggest in this letter that we move into her house. This was great news. For the baby's sake, she suggested, we should move in, and eventually the house would be mine anyway.

That evening I brought up the subject with Freddie. It sparked off our first royal battle. I was determined to move out of our slum while Freddie was horrified by the very idea of setting foot in the suburbs. 'Who in their right mind wants to live right out there?' he cried. 'Why, I'd never see me mates.'

I ignored him and systematically began to pack. Freddie was livid and lashed out. But instead of delivering the blow he intended, he kicked the door panel and made a great hole in it. With a roar of rage, he dashed out.

I was close to tears. I did not want to lose Freddie, but something had snapped inside me. I could bear these living conditions no longer. My mother's offer made it impossible for me to tolerate the constant shortage of hot water or the disgusting smell of the communal toilets on the landings. I continued packing, determined to leave.

To my surprise, Freddie returned home an hour later. He looked very contrite and seemed ready to accompany me. Who or what persuaded him to change his mind, I'll never know.

And so we moved into the house where I had grown up. How lovely it was to take a hot bath whenever I wanted, to relax on the settee by the fire, to sleep in a clean, airy room and to see the baby's nappies swinging on the washing line in the garden. I had never valued this home of mine before. I had never done any housework there, having always left that to my busy mother. Now I dusted and polished at every opportunity. No chore was too great for me.

Even Freddie seemed to settle in there at first. He loved the kitchen full of gadgets. There were almost as many as there had been at his mother's house.

But then, and I suppose inevitably, the boredom set in. Freddie began to talk about getting a job, which I approved of and encouraged him to do. He went off for hours on the trail of jobs but always came back late in the evenings quite plastered. Any fantasies I might have once had about changing his attitudes quickly evaporated.

My neighbours began to look very curiously at me when I passed them in the street. They rarely spoke to me in the shops and they certainly never dropped in as they used to when my friendly, cheerful mother lived there. And Freddie did not help, of course. Whenever he forgot his keys, which was often, he would loudly shout four-letter words up at the window in the middle of the night in order to wake me up. But he always woke up half the residents of our posh avenue as well.

Our living on the social security was a bit of an embarrassment to me in that area, too. I felt very ashamed about producing my allowance book at the local post office, and I hated anyone knowing that we lived on the state. I ignored old school pals and kept very much to myself. And I walked further on down that lonely road of mine.

Freddie had suddenly become more prosperous of late and now he often brought things home, either presents or good things to eat, like a leg of lamb for supper or chocolates for me. He had also taken to going up to London to hang out with his original pals. He would spend more time up there than I cared to recall. The sums of money increased. He bought flashy clothes and gear for himself and often handed me large wads of cash. I never asked any questions. I don't think it ever occurred to me. I suppose I assumed that a husband should provide and the wife should be happy for it. Anyway, with these lump sums he gave me, I opened a deposit account for Kevin.

Freddie would be out most nights now, returning in the early hours of the morning in a large car driven by a pal. With a squeal of brakes, the slamming of doors and hooter blaring, Freddie would be dropped off outside the house and he would saunter in noisily.

I began to lie awake listening out for the sound of the car in order to creep downstairs and open the door to prevent Freddie waking up the neighbours. On one particular night he was later than ever. It was two o'clock when I heard the squealing wheels and saw the headlights shining on the bedroom wall. The car seemed to stop just for a moment or two and then went speeding off with less noise than usual. I went downstairs very slowly and waited in the hall to see

Freddie's hand on the latch. But he did not come in. I waited a few more minutes. It seemed endless. But someone was out there. It *had* to be Freddie. Telling myself not to be silly, I slowly opened the door and peered out. There was a shape lying heavily against the hedge and grunting. It lifted its head, and I could see that it was indeed Freddie, just recognizable through the blood covering his face. 'Help me, help me,' he gasped. He reached out his arm and then dropped it as he passed out.

I knelt down and tried to staunch the blood that flowed from a wound on the side of his head. I tried in vain to pull him in over the doorstep but I was not strong enough. Weeping and panic-stricken, I ran inside and dailled for an ambulance. It never occurred to me as I did so that I was handing my own husband over to the law.

I could not leave the baby so Freddie had to go to hospital in the ambulance alone. For the best part of the night, I sat impotently beside the telephone. Come daylight, I rang the hospital to ask how Freddie was. The nurse sounded evasive to me. Freddie had slight concussion and cuts, she said, but otherwise he was all right.

With a great sense of relief, I got the baby dressed and went on the bus to the local hospital. Freddie was sitting up in bed with two black eyes and his head in a bandage. I got the biggest shock of my life. For there standing beside him was a policeman.

'You silly bitch!' scowled Freddie when he saw me. Then he ignored me and reached out his arms to hold his baby son. I did not stay long, I did not want to hear any more insults flying at me from Freddie's mouth. The young policeman looked at me sympathetically as Freddie accused me of being a traitor and causing him to be nicked.

He was right, of course. Feeling hurt and bewildered, I took Kevin in my arms and went home to my lonely abode.

Once he was fit to be moved, Freddie was transported back to prison on remand. I soon learned that he had been charged with robbery, having been involved in a bank robbery on that fateful night.

The bottom had fallen out of my world. What else could I have done? Everything was a mess. And to cap it all, before Freddie came up for trial, I realized that I was pregnant again.

The trial seemed to me to be a big farce. Everything moved so fast it was hard to follow what was going on exactly. And then I did a very foolish thing. The woman magistrate said: 'Would anyone like to speak up on behalf of this young man before I sum up?' And I leaped to my feet and stepped forward, determined to plead for my man.

And so that sour woman magistrate questioned me and in no time had tied me in knots. Every word I uttered seemed to make the situation worse. I had explained at great length how kind Freddie was to his wife and child, and how he often brought us presents.

The magistrate peered at me over her dark spectacles. 'And tell me,' she said, 'how did your husband have the means to buy all these kind presents for you?

He did not have a job at this time and you were receiving social security.'

I flushed bright red, realizing what a mistake I had made. I muttered and then quickly announced that I was pregnant. I don't know what I hoped to achieve by saying this, but it certainly did not help. The magistrate sighed audibly and removed those intimidating glasses. 'Oh, dear,' she said in a loud aside. 'They are always pregnant.'

It seemed to me that she then shot me a shrewd glance which told me that I was better off without Freddie. I was so confused by everything that went on in that court that I hardly heard the sentence: Five years.

'Thanks, mate,' Freddie called out to me as he was marched off in handcuffs. 'I might have got a suspended sentence if you hadn't insisted on saying your piece.'

I watched him disappear down to the cells and I knew that I did not love him as I thought I did.

All this happened several years ago. I am older and wiser now. I have a son at school and a daughter in nursery. I have grown up and feel in control of my life at last. My mother still lives abroad, so I am alone. But I intend to stay that way, even when Freddie comes out, for I prefer to rely on myself. It's safer that way.

An English Rose

Hetty Smith stood staring into the window of the travel agent. She had just finished an unappetizing lunch of hard-boiled-egg sandwiches and weak tea. She had eaten this at her desk but had then gone out for a walk to get some air.

Outside, the streets were busy. The traffic roared past, pedestrians hurried by chattering to each other and jostling others as they went. Hetty remained glued to the window of the travel agent, staring up at large coloured posters of snow-capped mountains and skiers in sunglasses, of pretty girls with long, slim, tanned bodies spread out on white beaches and surrounded by the bluest of skies and seas.

She breathed a deep sigh. What the hell did all these tourists come to London for when there was all this lovely scenery elsewhere? How wonderful it would be just to go abroad, she thought. Hetty had only left London once in her young life, and that was just to go to Hastings for the day. Yes, she would love to go abroad for a holiday. It might just be possible, she thought. Her company was going to pay its staff the half-yearly bonus next week. It might just be possible that she would have enough to treat herself.

But then Hetty thought about how her Aunt Esther would borrow some of that money to pay the rates, and how Hetty would want to treat all the kids and spend the rest on clothes. So no doubt the week after she would be broke again anyway.

As she thought about this, Hetty wrinkled her freckled nose, and chewed the ends of her long fair hair, a bad habit she was unaware of. Perhaps this year would be different, she thought. She would keep all this hard-earned money and go off to see those mountains this year. Yes, she owed it to herself and no one was going to stop her.

So Hetty swung her long legs over the step and marched into the office that promised so much travel and adventure.

A young man was sitting behind the polished counter. He was all teeth and eye glasses and he looked delighted to see Hetty, the first prospective customer of the day. It was a slack time of year so he was particularly eager to please.

'I want to go abroad,' stated Hetty. 'Somewhere nice.'

The young man reached into a drawer and pulled out a batch of colour brochures. 'You can go anywhere you desire, madam. Your heart's desire is here – Italy, Spain, Yugoslavia, Austria – anything you want.' With his white teeth flashing, the young man launched into his sales patter.

'Cut the chat,' snapped Hetty impatiently. 'I wanna

go where those mountains are.' She pointed to a poster on the wall. 'And I want to go next week.'

'Very good choice,' agreed the travel salesman. 'We can offer you reduced rates at this time of the year, too.'

'Well, where is it?' asked Hetty. 'And how much does it cost to get there?'

'Ah, the Italian Alps,' said the man with a dramatic sweep of his arm. 'It's very lovely there. You will be flying, I presume.'

'Well, I ain't got no wings, so I'll need a plane,' Hetty retorted, irritated by his condescending manner.

The arrangements were made and a five-pound deposit was paid for Hetty's trip to Italy. She was to fly to Milan and then a coach would take her to that grand lake surrounded by snow-capped mountains.

The agreement made, Hetty returned to her office and typewriter feeling very pleased with herself.

The other girls in the office were impressed and amazed. 'You're joking, Hetty,' they said. 'You're going to Italy on your own at this time of year?'

'I am, too,' replied the truculent Hetty, 'and no one ain't going to stop me, either.'

Aunt Esther was appalled at the news and nagged Hetty all week. She stood arms akimbo as Hetty ironed her clothes and packed them in a suitcase.

'You must be going barmy,' scoffed Aunt Esther. 'Why can't you wait till the summer and then go to Butlins, or somewhere normal?'

But Hetty, with her blonde hair in rollers, continued to iron her clothes placidly. 'I said I'm going, and that's that,' she said quietly.

'Well, let's hope the white slavers don't get yer,' her aunt retorted. Needless to say, Aunt Esther had never been abroad and never intended to go, either.

Settled in her aeroplane seat, Hetty breathed a sigh of relief when the No Smoking sign went off at last. She was off and away on a ten-day dash to do just as she pleased.

Her hotel and meals were all paid for and she had twenty pounds spending money. It was not a fortune but the chances were that she would meet a bloke who would treat her and help to stretch her money a bit. She looked around at the other passengers on the plane. There were some bald-headed businessmen with their secretaries and a few retired couples. Not much hope there.

Although her nose was in a book, Hetty's mind was more on thoughts of getting a rich lover. It was just as well that she had brought along her supply of pills. After all, you never knew your luck, she told herself.

She was not a bad girl, Hetty, just a victim of circumstance. At school she had been taught about the facts of life but not about the real difficulties of sex. She was not, for instance, told how to hang on to your virginity when you are full of vodka and with a boy you are crazy about.

That particular boy had been poor little Jim who then got himself killed on a motorbike a few weeks later. That had been a shock to poor Hetty. Luckily she did not get pregnant and then she went on the pill. Then that last rotter turned out to be married, and strung her along. After a long time, she was just coming out of a man-hating phase and ready to meet someone nice. She might meet someone on this holiday. After all, there had to be someone somewhere who wanted a wife with long legs and freckles, and who couldn't cook hot water.

It was not long before the Fasten Seat-belts sign lighted up again. The plane was about to land. Within thirty minutes, Hetty had collected her luggage and was standing in the queue to pass through Customs and passport control.

She thought about her money, now changed to Italian lire, stashed away in her suitcase. She hoped it was safe.

A short fat official looked at her passport. 'Harriet Smith,' he read out in a loud voice.

Hetty blushed and looked away. She hated to be called Harriet. What a name! She liked to forget that she had been christened Harriet, though she had been reminded only last week when she got her passport.

She snatched back her passport and pushed on past. She was feeling very confused. There were so many people pushing and shoving and yakking in a foreign language. She wandered outside the airport and stood there looking rather lost.

A tall, dark young man came towards her. He smiled in a friendly way. 'May I help you?' he asked in good English, and took hold of her suitcase. 'Follow me,' he continued. 'I'll get you a taxi to your hotel.'

Follow him? Well, that was easier said than done. Hetty ran after the man, her high heels catching in the cracks in the pavement. Crowds of people milled around. Hetty tried desperately to keep the young man in sight but then his tall figure disappeared, along with her suitcase and all her money.

Hetty could not believe what had happened to her. 'Why, you silly fool,' she muttered. 'You come all this way to get conned! Well, Hetty Smith, what are you going to do now?'

The sun blazed down on her head. As she stood there looking from left to right, wondering what to do, a taxi drew up. She jingled the few lira coins in her coat pocket. She might have just enough to get to her hotel. And then she should inform the police.

The taxi driver opened the door for her and nodded as Hetty repeated the name of the hotel she was booked into for the night.

Hetty settled herself into the back seat and the car drove off as she noticed another person sitting in the front passenger seat. He was a little fat man who could have been a brother of that horrible passport-control officer who called out her name so loudly. This man was wearing a smart dark suit and sported a white carnation in his buttonhole. He smiled and nodded at her but said nothing.

The taxi stopped outside a big hotel. Hetty was sure that it was not the hotel she had asked for. Forgetting to pay the driver (though he did not protest), Hetty ran up the steps of the hotel to the reception desk.

'My name is Miss Smith. Have I a room booked here?' she asked.

To her amazement, the receptionist nodded. 'Harriet Smith? Yes, indeed.'

In no time at all, Hetty was being escorted to the lift. But Hetty was quite bewildered. This was a very posh hotel and she was sure that the travel agent had made a mistake. Still, if a room was booked for her, it must be right.

She tried to explain to the bell boy about her luggage. 'Can you tell me where I should go to try and find it?' she asked. But his reply was nonsensical. '*Si, si, signorina*,' he said, unlocking a room door and leading her in. With a polite bow, he left.

When Hetty turned and saw the room she was standing in, she knew there was something seriously amiss. 'Blimey!' she exclaimed looking at the high wall-mirrors and soft carpets. There were antiques everywhere, and by the window a small round table had been set with silver cutlery ready for a meal for two. Crikey, thought Hetty, I'd better get out of here before his lordship arrives. As she backed away towards the door, there was a gentle tap from outside.

Hetty gingerly opened the door to see in front of her the little fat man who had ridden in the front seat of the taxi.

The man bowed deeply. 'I have come to help you,' he said in perfect English.

'Well thank God for that,' exclaimed Hetty. 'I was getting worried. I'm in the wrong hotel and I've lost all my luggage.'

The man ignored her words and waddled through the door past her. 'Sit down, Miss Smith,' he said cheerfully. 'Your luggage will be here soon. Now we shall dine. You must be tired and travel weary.'

Hetty was dumbstruck. This has to be *Candid Camera*, or something, she thought, or a wonderfully funny dream. She sat down at the perfectly laid table and accepted the glass of wine the fat man was holding out to her.

Yes, it's a film, decided Hetty as a young waiter wheeled in a trolley of delicious-smelling food under silver covers.

Hetty was very hungry and she now tucked in heartily, savouring the tasty food with glee. She did not ask what anything was, and did not care. And after the third glass of wine, she had even stopped worrying about her problems; they did not seem so bad somehow.

As the waiter cleared the table, Hetty and the fat man sat down on a richly covered divan. Now Hetty was getting nervous. What's this old geezer after, she wondered, I don't want him pawing me.

The man was pulling out his wallet. 'I know that you need money,' he said. 'And I have a proposition for you.'

'No thanks,' cried Hetty, leaping to her feet. 'I'm not what you think. I'm not one of those.'

The fat man looked distressed. 'No, wait,' he begged. 'Wait, my beautiful English rose, do not go until you have listened to me.'

Hetty was startled by his continuing politeness and good manners. She blinked at him. 'What do you want of me?' she asked, wide-eyed and scared.

'To stay here for one night,' he replied. 'And not with me, but with my friend.' He said this in a strange, matter-of-fact way.

Hetty decided to go along with this. She looked sideways at him. 'How much you going to give me, then?'

The man pulled out a huge wad of ten-pound notes.

Hetty looked at the money with great interest. She wondered what she would be expected to do and why she had been picked out. In her head rang her aunt's warning of white slavers. 'Why me?' she whispered.

The fat man nodded. 'I am a very well-read man,' he said, 'and I have always been taken by the character Harriet Smith, the quintessential English rose that the writer Jane Austen wrote of.' He began to quote: ' "A girl of seventeen . . . a very pretty girl. She was short, plump and fair, with a fine bloom, blue eyes, light hair, regular features and a look of great sweetness . . ." ' The fat man smiled. 'You are not plump, Miss Smith, but otherwise you fit the description remarkably well.'

Hetty blushed scarlet. The quotation from Jane Austen's *Emma* meant nothing to her. She had left school at sixteen and read little or no English literature. But the fact that it was her name, Harriet, that had got her into this spot made her hate it more than ever.

'Well, get to the point,' she said. 'What do I have to do for a hundred quid?' She had by now resigned herself to the situation. No one knew her here, so why should she care? And besides, what a smashing time she would have on a hundred quid . . .

The fat man got to his feet and opened a door she had not noticed. It led to another room but there, near the doorway, stood a tall, well-built young man. Long silky curls hung around his head. His large dark eyes looked tired and there seemed to be something wrong with his lip. But he was very handsome and when he smiled, as he did now, she could see a row of dazzling white teeth; he was devastating. Oh boy, thought Hetty. That's more like it!

The young man bowed low. 'I, who am about to die, salute you,' he said. He spoke in a soft slow voice which made shivers run up and down Hetty's spine. He gave the impression of being drunk or drugged, in some way. Certainly he was a little high. But cor, he was certainly smashing, thought Hetty. She would not mind sleeping with him for nothing!

The fat man started to introduce Hetty and the young man but such an act of politeness was unnecessary. The wine and the spicy scent that wafted from the handsome man drew Hetty towards him as a needle is drawn to a magnet.

'She is perfect,' the young man whispered. 'A beautiful fair English rose, just as Jane Austen described.'

Hetty giggled. 'You're a fast worker,' she murmured as he pressed his lips on hers and kissed her.

His lips were hot and dry. Slowly travelling down her neck, they reached her breasts. Hetty was used to fighting off the roughnecks in London, but this left her feeling trapped, limp and very willing, as he pressed against her.

Hetty was vaguely aware of the fat man tactfully withdrawing from the room, but everything else was oblivion. The young man led her gently to the divan where they both sat down. He made no more approaches towards her but just sat smoking and staring at her.

Hetty curled up her long legs and snuggled up beside him. She stared at his swollen and scarred bottom lip and reached up to touch it. It was the only feature that marred this virile beauty. 'What happened to your lip?' She caressed his shiny hair.

The man looked down at her and took a drag on his cigarette. There was a strange remoteness in his eyes still. He ignored her question but spoke in a quiet musical voice. 'This is my last night on earth. At dawn I die.'

Hetty just suppressed a giggle. 'Yeah, well we all have to die,' she joked. The man was obviously a bit loopy but what the heck, she thought. He can get away with it with those looks.

The man smiled. 'You think I joke? Well, let that be so. Forget tomorrow, and now let's drink, my English beauty.'

Between them they finished the wine and then ordered champagne. Well lubricated, they danced to soft music. The world stood still as the man held Hetty in his arms and danced closer and closer.

Hetty never did remember how she got undressed but never in her life would she forget the hours just before dawn when they made love on the bed over and over again. They both seemed insatiable.

'I wish I could go on living and go on making love to you forever,' he whispered.

Hetty smiled peacefully. Never had she felt so peaceful and content. Her eyes closed and she drifted off to sleep dreaming of flying carpets.

She awoke suddenly, aware of a strange presence

in the room. It was light outside and standing over her head was a nasty-looking man with narrow slits for eyes.

'If you value your life, don't make a sound,' he hissed.

This is a nightmare, she thought. But she knew that it was not. She shut her eyes and then opened them again to take another look at the mean face. Reaching over to the other side of the bed, she felt it was empty. And then she saw her lover standing by the doorway. He was flanked by two soldiers and his hands were handcuffed.

He smiled at her. 'Thank you, English rose,' he called. 'Farewell.'

And the door was quietly closed as the two soldiers led him out. 'You can sit up now, but don't scream,' said the mean-looking man beside her. 'Lover boy's gone. You won't be having the pleasure of him again.'

Hetty was too afraid to sit up. She just lay on her back like a scared animal, shivering in terror.

Suddenly there was the noise of a car outside. The man looked out of the window and then quickly backed out of the door.

The moment he was gone, Hetty began to scream. She found her voice with a vengeance. Immediately the little fat man rushed in from the next door room. He had tears streaming down his face. 'Hush,' he called. 'It's no good to scream, we cannot save Ahmed. It's the will of Allah.'

He sat beside her bed and began to blubber like a

baby. Hetty joined in, howling loudly and longing to be back in her warm bed at home.

By midday Hetty was feeling much better. Her suitcase had been returned to her, she was freshly bathed and now wore a clean dress. She sat in the hotel dining room lunching with Pierre, the fat man, as he was called.

'I and my honourable family will be eternally grateful to you for last night's work,' he said.

Hetty smiled and nodded. With one thousand pounds in her bag, she felt quite buoyant. 'I still don't know what this is all about,' she said. 'I came for a holiday and it all seemed to turn into a damn film set.'

Pierre grimaced. 'I'm afraid it's no film, Miss Smith, it's true life. This morning a young man died for his country. He was a brave youth – and my own nephew. Now you must forget all that you have seen and heard and go and enjoy your holiday.'

Hetty could tell that he was not going to tell her what was going on. 'Yes, I must get to the mountains,' she said, 'as I *did* come here for a special holiday.'

Pierre nodded. 'Your trip up there will be arranged. And I have a companion for you . . .' Hetty looked interested at the thought of another lover, and another thousand quid. Well, that would be too good to be true. Then she felt guilty at her greediness and thought of the mysterious Ahmed and their night of passion.

A young girl of about thirteen joined them. She had long plaits and olive skin and wore a rich blue dress over flowing trousers. 'This is my own child, Mina,' said Pierre. 'She will go with you and look after you.'

Hetty eyed Mina, who gave her a flashing smile. 'She does not speak English, only French and Arabic, but she can understand you. She will go with you to the lake,' Pierre continued.

'But I thought my job was for one night only,' Hetty said.

'Let me detain you a while longer,' pleaded Pierre. 'If the great God Allah wills that you bear Ahmed's son, I will have to ask you to stay until the child is born, for the honour of my family. You will be taken good care of and, in the event of failure, your passport will be returned and I shall escort you personally to the plane. And for your trouble I shall give you another five hundred pounds.'

Hetty looked dismayed. She had to pretend there was a chance. She dared not tell him she was on the pill. She would have to stay at least three weeks. What would her aunt say?

Pierre squeezed her hand. 'Be patient with us, my dear,' he said. 'And be honoured that you were chosen to be Ahmed's beautiful English rose.'

And so, not mentioning the contraceptive pill, Hetty allowed herself to be escorted to a car with Mina and whisked off to a posh hotel in a swanky mountain resort miles from anywhere. The pretty brown-skinned Mina waited on her constantly and sat in the shade while Hetty roasted herself in the mountain sun. And in the evening, Hetty would consume delicious food and wine and smoke French cigarettes while Mina sewed or played the sitar.

Hetty quickly became very bored. After two weeks,

a cockney voice would have been manna from Heaven. But she had to keep up the pretence and stick it out in order to earn the extra money. At last her period started and she informed Mina. Mina rang her father and spoke rapidly in Arabic down the telephone.

The next day, they travelled back to Milan to be met at the hotel by a sad-looking Pierre.

'And do not forget Ahmed,' said Pierre as he escorted Hetty to the airport. He handed her another wad of bank notes and a bundle of newspapers to read.

It was the first time Hetty had seen an English paper since she had left London. As the plane rose above the clouds she opened one of them up. On the front page Ahmed's sad face stared out at her. Underneath was the headline: 'ARAB TERRORIST EXECUTED BY ISRAELIS'. The article went on to say a French-born Arab terrorist had been murdered in a Milan suburb. It was believed that this was in connection with the blowing-up of Israeli aeroplanes at Rome Airport last year. It was regarded as some sort of reprisal. Hetty read on to learn that Ahmed was the son of a great Arab leader and that his death was mourned by the whole Arab community.

Hetty realized that tears were streaming down her cheeks. So it was all true. Poor, brave Ahmed. He knew that he was going to his death, that the Israelis were on his trail. His last request had been for a woman, and fate made sure that it was she who was chosen.

She felt a surge of pride in her heart but also a sudden stab of sorrow that she was not to be mother of a patriot's son.

The next Monday morning, a sun-tanned Hetty was back at the typewriter. 'You took yer time coming home,' said nosy Miss Clark.

'Well, I had a job out there,' replied Hetty.

'A job? What did you do?' The other girls looked very interested.

Hetty looked down at the long suede boots she had just bought and smiled at the thought of all the money in her bank account. 'I was waiting,' she replied with a grin.

'You mean, you was a waitress?' said Miss Clark.

Hetty smiled enigmatically. 'You could say that,' she said quietly, 'you could say that.'

A Foreign Romance

My name is Riena de Fries. I am Dutch but from a very young age I had always had a yearning to go to England. For many years I had in my possession a small passport photograph of a sad-eyed, dark-haired lady whom Uncle Jan had brought home after the war, a long time ago, before I was born. Members of my family still talked in hushed voices of this errant lady who had quickly fled back home again across the North Sea, leaving poor Uncle Jan heartbroken. He was so distraught that he never recovered. Even now he was not married and the dim, dark secret of his lost love was locked up tightly in the hearts of our close-knit family.

As a child, in the privacy of my own little hide-out under the old wooden beams in the loft, I would frequently gaze at that faded photograph and weave fantastic tales centred on this dark lady and the land of her birth, called England. Most of my life I had lived with my grandparents. My parents owned a small cargo vessel and my mother accompanied my father on most of his trips. But I was a happy child and my life with Oma and Opa was certainly a contented one. I was, however, often lonely on our small island in the Zuider Zee.

When I was seventeen, I attended a college in town each weekday, and at weekends I wandered along the white sandy beaches with our two dogs for company. I watched the dogs chase wild fowl or each other with carefree abandon, or I idled the time away down at the quayside listening to the gossip and chatter of the fisherwomen dressed in their stiffened skirts, with embroidered aprons and snow-white lace caps. It was always fun when we gathered together to welcome the homecoming fishermen. But looking out at the sea, I often wished that I could sprout wings and fly as freely as the white gulls that swooped over the bay.

I kept my dreams to myself. Oma and Opa were devoted to me, their only granddaughter, and I would never disobey them or do anything to upset them. But, as I became more restless, it became clear to me that I would have to broach the subject. I chose one cool evening when we were sitting outside the cottage, my grandmother and I both sewing, and Opa sat in his wooden chair smoking a pipe. I took a deep breath and spoke the words I had rehearsed so many times in the privacy of my own room.

'Oma and Opa, I want to go to England for the vacation.'

Oma paused in her sewing. She lifted her white head and looked at me with those inscrutable ice-blue eyes. There was a shocked silence. Opa removed the pipe from his mouth. His stern brown eyes, which could suddenly twinkle like a star, surveyed me for a silent moment. Then he chuckled. 'Zooo! So our little bird wants to fly from the nest.'

'She will do no such thing!' declared Oma crossly. 'Riena *must* stay here to finish her schooling. Then it is for her parents to decide.'

'But, Oma,' I pleaded. 'I can go *with* my school. We will travel in a party and be chaperoned by our teachers. And it is only for two weeks.'

'Oh, a holiday,' grumbled Oma. 'Why didn't you explain properly?'

Then my grandparents began a crossfire of conversation in their local dialect, which I always found too difficult to follow. I felt quite upset as I watched them intently. I was so fond of them and could not bear to have them quarrel over me. Then quite suddenly it ceased. Opa again lit up his *meerschaum* pipe, and Oma reached over to pick up her sewing. Through the rising cloud of tobacco smoke, Opa gave me a prodigious wink, and I knew I had got my way.

One day in August, flushed with excitement, I boarded the cross-channel ferry with a party of fellow students. We all wore bright, hand-knitted jerseys, carried smart travelling bags and chattered like starlings. My grandmother had fussed over this trip right up to the moment of my departure. Even as I waved goodbye, she instructed me on my behaviour. 'No strong drink, no smoking, no pills of any description and *never* be alone in male company.'

So with the permission from the old folk and a cheque from my parents, I had at last obtained my heart's desire.

The crossing was stormy and the North Sea looked cold and grey. Many of the other students ate and drank too much and got terribly seasick. Since I came from a seafaring family, there was no nonsense like that for me. I sat in the saloon with a book by Charles Dickens on my knee, but I was too excited to read. I was heading for England!

We were to be the guests of a small town called Rochester in Kent, in a hostel not far from Dickens's home. There is an ancient castle in this historic town, a wide river and a long bridge. In many ways it was not unlike the small town back home where I attended college each day, but I soon missed the peaceful beauty of the canals. The amount of traffic on its way to the coast and the busy narrow streets scared the wits out of me, a rural-bred Dutch girl. But Rochester was hardly a lively place and the more adventurous of my classmates soon made their way to London, where they spent the days and nearly all the nights living it up in that swinging city. My own first trip to London had been so confusing that I decided to spend the rest of my time in Rochester. 'Let Riena be,' said my classmates. 'She's a bit of a drag up in town.'

I did not mind. I was used to being on my own so, as a solitary figure, I went alone to visit the museum, the library, the famous castle and the ancient cathedral. I made several trips to Dickens's House in the main street and enjoyed standing and staring at that black-and-white half-timbered structure. It seemed amazing that it was so old.

Having absorbed all this English culture, I would walk down to the river to sit under the ivy-clad walls of the old castle, watching the milky river as it flowed on its way to the sea. I wrote postcards home, telling them what a lovely time I was having, and then I would read my book for a while, or leave it in my lap as I let my dreams flow in my head.

Every day at about two o'clock, I noticed a tall youth walked nonchalantly over the bridge. He always wore faded jeans and had his hands stuffed deep into his raincoat pockets.

I watched him with interest each day as he walked the length of the bridge, then leaned on the old iron framework to look calmly down at the river for a while. After that, he would sit on the seat nearby, with his long legs spread out in front of him and a far-away expression on his face. He would stay there till about half-past three, when he would get to his feet and in the same leisurely manner go back over the bridge and disappear out of sight. I watched him intently and thought how neat his hair was. It was red-brown and cut very short. I also liked his skin, which was fair and freckled.

Occasionally the youth would glance in my direction. This always made me panic. I would look away and cast my eyes down but my heart would be beating fast. How I longed to talk to him. My English was perfect, and I would dearly have loved to hold a conversation with this boy in his own mother tongue. Overwhelmed with bashfulness and nervousness, I could never find the courage to communicate. But then fate took a hand.

One such day, as the English weather often does, it suddenly changed. A cold wind drifted down river, whipping up the dry dust and dead leaves, and whirled them round like a miniature tornado. I put my hands to my face in fear of losing my spectacles, and the book slid from my lap. The boy stepped forward and retrieved it smartly. He looked at the cover. 'Charles Dickens,' he remarked, in a voice that had a very flat intonation. 'Well, that's English. I thought you were one of those foreign students who are staying in town.'

I looked straight back at him. His eyes were flecked with green, just like that muddy river. 'I am,' I said in my perfect school-room English. 'I am from Friesland in the Netherlands.'

'Is this all you can find to do?' he asked, indicating the book and the bench. 'You're here every day.'

I shrugged. 'But I like it down here,' I protested.

The sun came out at the very moment that he smiled. It was a wide infectious smile. 'That's funny,' he said, 'so do I. I hang about down here nearly every afternoon.'

We walked along the river bank. The boy was very easy to talk to, which must have been why I managed to conquer my shyness without any trouble.

We stood on the bridge and watched the small boats battling against the tide.

'Until I came here,' he said, 'I had never left the big city. I could not believe so much open space existed. Sometimes, I think I'll never ever go back to London.'

Slyly I admired his straight profile, his even white teeth, and the way the sun brought out the red glints in his hair. My heart behaved in an extraordinary manner, thumping madly, completely out of control. My new friend was so charming and I felt so perfectly at ease with him.

Thus my holiday had only just begun. We met at the

same spot every afternoon. Sometimes we walked through the town, sometimes we just sat idly by the river swapping stories of our school-days. He said his name was Robert but he liked to be called Bob. He was happy to talk of his childhood but he had little to say about what he did now, here in Rochester. I noticed too that he got edgy at about three o'clock. Otherwise, the time passed on golden wings.

One wonderful afternoon we hitch-hiked out of town and sat in the long grass in a large Kentish orchard. Huge red apples simply dripped from the wide-spreading branches. The birds sang loudly. Otherwise, all was peace and beauty. Bob gently took off my spectacles and unbraided my long hair. 'There,' he said, 'you look really smashing.' Fresh, strong lips pressed down on to mine. The birds sang even more sweetly and there was a scent of newly mown hay in the air as Cupid shot his arrow.

'I don't think a boy has ever kissed you before,' he whispered tenderly. When I blushed, he kissed me again and again. Unused to petting, I suddenly became scared as his lovemaking grew more passionate. 'It's all right, little Dutchy,' he reassured me in a gentle voice, 'I would not harm a lovely girl like you.'

And true to his word, he did not force me. We just kissed and cuddled.

On the way back to Rochester, Bob was silent and seemed unhappy. Inexperienced as I was, I was worried. I had no idea of how to console him.

'I must be the unluckiest bloke alive,' he complained enigmatically, 'to meet a girl like you.'

When we parted, he said 'It's goodbye from now on, Dutchy'.

Tears sprang into my eyes. I was positively crestfallen. Bob held me close. 'Now don't cry, it's not anything you have done or not done,' he assured me. 'It's been great being with you and talking to you.' With a friendly kiss, he left, his long legs speeding him over the bridge.

I stared disconsolately after him, the flutter of excitement within me like a little bird trying to escape. The day had been so wonderful, I was not going to spoil it. Bob would be back tomorrow, I was sure of that. I went back to the hostel to dream sweet dreams.

But for the next two days I sadly watched and waited in vain for the sight of Bob's tall slim figure coming over the bridge. The weather had changed. It had become cold and rainy. But for the hungry gulls, the esplanade was deserted. I was so filled with remorse. It was entirely my fault that he did not come. I had driven him away. How I longed for a glimpse of that sunny smile! I conjured him up in my head again and again. The terrifying thought of never meeting him again made my eyes fill with tears and my mouth tremble.

I sat there alone in the shelter seat, huddled in the corner against the elements, and looking up at the bridge. With its leering stone lions, it suddenly seemed grotesque.

I was startled out of my misery by the sound of a coach hooter. A voice shouted to me in Dutch. It was my teacher. 'Why on earth are you sitting out there alone?' she demanded. 'Come on, get in,' she said, impatiently opening the coach door. 'We are going to visit a stately home.'

Reluctantly, I gave in to authority, but I worried that Bob might turn up by the river and I would not be there.

The visit to the grand house failed to interest me; I felt lethargic and depressed. Not even my merry class-mates could cheer me up. At five o'clock we waited in a group to climb back into the coach to take us back to town. Down the straight narrow road came an open truck. It slowed down at the bend in the road. Inside, sitting in the back, were a group of youths. They looked tired and dusty and wore the same faded blue overalls. Raising my eyes to stare at them, I found myself gazing straight into the greeny eyes of my friend Bob. He stared back at me but he showed no sign of recognition. In fact, he just looked cold and indifferent from his seat in the back of the lorry.

Involuntarily, I raised my hand to wave, and then dropped it immediately. 'Someone you know in there?' asked one of my fellow students curiously.

Sadly, I shook my head.

'Look at those poor devils,' remarked the coach driver. 'Prisoners, they are. They've been working in the fields all day. Bet they don't 'arf fancy a cup of tea.'

I could hardly believe my ears. So that was the mystery of Bob! He was a prisoner but he left the work party every day to idle his time by the river. So he was a criminal! At night he was shut up behind high walls. How confused and unhappy I felt! And tomorrow I would be on my way home and would never see him again. It was almost too much to bear.

But bear it I had to. I returned home with my group. Uncle Jan was there to meet me off the ferry. 'England does not seem to have done you a lot of good,' he remarked. 'In fact it looks as if you have got the lemon complexion of the English.'

Once home in Friesland my spirits did not improve. I felt like a wilted flower deprived of light. I became very thin because I ate so little, and every day I would sit pensively in the small courtyard watching the canal flow past. Oma's wrinkled face looked anxiously in my direction but she said nothing. Opa would look up from behind his newspaper and occasionally mutter, 'The dogs are bursting for exercise.'

'Can't be bothered,' I always moodily answered.

At night, as they sat under the warm red lampshade at the round polished table, I could hear my grandparents discussing their problem grandchild. From within the cupboard in the wall bed, I strained my ears to listen. "Tis not our Riena any more,' Oma protested. 'I never wanted her to visit a foreign shore – look how it upset the life of our own Jan.'

'Zooo, Mama, it could just be growing pains,' retorted Opa. 'But I will admit that she's become as broody as a young hen.'

Eventually time and circumstances solved my grandparents' worries. After all her years on the water, my mother had decided to come ashore, a term used by water-folk to distinguish them from the farming families. Opa and Oma had originally been water-folk. They raised seven children, and every one was born in the canal boat. But then old age had driven them ashore. Now my parents too were feeling their age and were going to move into a new home in Amsterdam and wanted me to join them at last.

It was very hard to say goodbye to my dear grandparents. They had cared for me so long. With her soft white hair blowing in the wind and tears pouring down her wrinkled cheeks, Oma waved goodbye. Opa escorted me to the train station. I kept glancing fondly at his stern face, at the heavy moustache which veiled his lips so that you could never be sure if he was smiling or not. How I loved those deep brown eyes, which often suddenly twinkled to betray the humour within. How very much I was going to miss them! But at the same time I was relieved to be going somewhere different. I had felt so hurt, lonely and restless since my trip to England that it was an infinite relief to have a complete change.

'I'll bring Oma to visit you in the spring,' Opa promised.

As the train sped towards Amsterdam, I made plans. I would not finish my studies at college, I decided. I might get a job in the city. There was a good chance of that, I thought. The Common Market had created a demand for English-speaking typists.

I found my thoughts wandering back to that sunny orchard in Kent, the bright red apples on green grass, the soft kisses that wet my lips. I was gripped once more by that hurt feeling. No, Bob did not love me. He had completely ignored me when I saw him go past in the back of the prison truck. Besides, he was a criminal. I had to forget him.

My tall, bright mother met me at the station with a lovely smile on her face. She chattered excitedly as a newly-wed about her new house. All my mother's married life had been spent aboard the cargo vessel and before that her childhood had been on a canal barge. It was little wonder that she was so thrilled at owning a house. I think that excited her more than the return of her only child.

After a few days my father left for the deep sea once more. I loved my steady, seafaring papa, and found now that I often got bored by my excitable, house-proud mama. Luckily, when my mother's incessant painting and cleaning depressed me, I was able to visit Uncle Jan who lived on a boat in Amsterdam harbour. He was, according to my family, lazy and a drunkard. He was certainly not much of a skipper, and he seldom sailed from harbour these days. It was to Uncle Jan in his derelict boat that I took my broken heart.

Uncle Jan was leaning against the lobster pots when I arrived one day. He was a short, square man. He wore baggy pants and wooden clogs, and a peaked skipper's cap was perched on the back of his head where his dull red hair grew quite abundantly. At the front of his head, his hair had receded to the point of baldness. Uncle Jan's eyes were almost identical to Opa's, though they were perhaps a little more sorrowful and certainly more red veined from too much alcohol. But they did light up in the same manner as Opa when he smiled. He was always to be found at this spot close to the tavern.

Being a bachelor, Uncle Jan did not care a jot for anyone. But he liked me. When he saw me approaching, he came forward to greet me. I smiled at him.

'Oh, that's better, little one. A nice smile for me today – nothing like that lemon face you brought home from your holidays in England. Come aboard, and we'll have some coffee.'

We took that precarious path down the narrow gang-planks which separated the many craft in this cosmopolitan harbour. Hundreds of small seacraft were anchored close together, bobbing up and down on the water. Many had families living on them, and old folk, and women with toddlers on leashes walked these planks daily. The whole area jumped with life. Washing fluttered in the breeze, radios blared, children played. It was a hive of human interest and activity. Many of the boats were very smart with plant pots in the windows, net curtains, shining brass and vivid paintwork. A few, like Uncle Jan's, were almost devoid of paint.

The decks of Uncle Jan's boat were littered with ropes and rubbish, and the funnel belched smoke from the old stove that burned driftwood. It had once been a very smart vessel in which Uncle Jan had sailed off to foreign climes. But now it reflected his disillusioned frame of mind and lay rusting in the harbour.

I washed up the dishes in the grimy sink and tidied up the messy cabin while Uncle Jan made some coffee. Then he lit his pipe and put his feet up on a seat, while I cuddled close, ignoring his oil-stained trousers. 'May I ask you something, Uncle Jan?' I said.

'As long as it's not for money,' he joked.

'I wondered . . .' I felt timid at asking him, 'if you liked England.'

He thought for a moment. 'I had to go,' he replied. 'The Nazis took over and I wasn't going to sail for them.'

I sighed. 'It must have been so romantic in those days.'

Uncle Jan laughed. 'Surely you mean dangerous! I was damned lucky to get back alive.'

'Tell me about it all,' I whispered.

Uncle Jan took his pipe out of his mouth and stared curiously at me. 'Why don't you tell me about your trip?' he said, gently. 'Tell me what happened to you in England. That is what you want to do, isn't it?'

'I fell in love, over there,' I blurted out. I felt so shy.

'Good,' said Uncle Jan with a grin.

'But he was in prison,' I added faintly.

Uncle Jan revealed his nicotine-stained teeth as he threw back his head and roared with laughter.

'Oh, don't, Uncle Jan!' I placed my head pathetically on his lap and he stroked my hair.

'Come on, let's have it all from the beginning,' he said gently. And so I confided in Uncle Jan and told him of my tale of love. I felt quite tearful as I described how I had last seen Bob in that truck, packed in with the others like cattle. 'What do you think, Uncle Jan? I simply can't forget him. Oh, why am I so soft?'

'Not so soft, love, you just had a natural brush with love,' Uncle Jan said. 'Like a little flower that has been dusted with pollen, it will blow away in the wind. And the next time you will be more sure of your feelings.'

'Would it be terribly wrong to love a criminal?' I asked.

Uncle Jan shook his head. 'If your friend was so

young, he would have been at an approved school, not a prison. If I can remember correctly, most of my crew of cockney lads graduated from approved schools, but fine sailor lads they all were, I take my hat off to them.' With a dramatic gesture, he raised his old skipper's cap high.

I had to giggle. 'Thank you, Uncle Jan,' I said. 'You always cheer me up.'

'You will meet another boy and one of your own kind,' he consoled me.

We sat for a while in silence. Then I spoke. 'Why did you not get married, Uncle Jan?'

'Why? You little vixen!' exclaimed Uncle Jan, pretending to be shocked. 'You know why! Have not the family been gossiping about it for years?'

'I'm sorry,' I murmured. I felt a bit shamefaced at intruding on his private life.

'It does not matter,' he said, 'but I will tell you that I know from experience that life has a way of healing all scars. I once loved a woman who was married. I could not have her and I never wanted anyone else. That's all I can say.'

And no more was said. As for me, having confided my secret to Uncle Jan, I immediately began to feel better. I began to feel more confident and found it easier to smile. And whenever that uncomfortable yearning feeling returned, I dismissed it. I worked hard at the office and studied in the evenings.

In this way that winter passed quite quickly. The canals were frozen over, so the boats stayed in harbour until the spring came round again. Opa and Oma came up to town on a visit early in the new year, and the family gathered to eat, drink schnapps and gossip. Again Uncle Jan was the subject of discussion. 'The old fool is talking of repairing his boat and sailing up the Rhine in that old tub,' remarked my father.

'Why! It would be disastrous,' agreed my grandmother.

The next day I took a trip down to the harbour to find out what my impossible but dear uncle was up to.

It was a clear, cold day with a blue sky and crisp air. I felt light-hearted and wonderfully happy for some unknown reason. The huddle of vessels in the harbour lay silent and peaceful. Uncle Jan was not on board his boat. There were paint pots and tar pots lying about, and it looked as if he really had some intentions of repairing and repainting his craft. But the fact that he was not there suggested that he had found the tavern more alluring. So I went down to the quay to wait until my uncle emerged from the tavern.

A little bridge crossed the canal that led to the tavern, and as I sat waiting and watching, my mind roamed back to another bridge miles across the sea where I had waited for Bob. To my surprise, my heart did not hurt. Patiently I waited for Uncle Jan, not daring to approach that tavern full of drinking skippers. As I sat there I noticed a tall figure step on to the bridge. He walked a little way and then stood at the centre and looked down into the water. I squinted into the sunlight. He seemed familiar . . . but it was impossible!

I had to be dreaming. I got up and walked to the end of the bridge. At that moment, the young man stopped staring down into the water and continued on over the bridge. We met at the bottom step. My heart was beating so fast that I was breathless. I almost fainted. The world stood still as I looked again at that wide grin, those green eyes and that reddish hair. It was my Bob, in the flesh.

'Why, Riena!' he exclaimed. 'Little Dutchy! At last I have found you.'

I held out my hands to him. 'Bob! Oh, Bob! What are you doing here?' I asked.

We stood close together, hands clasped tight.

'I can't believe my luck,' he said. 'Why, I've looked everywhere for you. I've even been to that godforsaken island you told me about. I tracked down your grand-parents' house but no one was there. Then someone suggested that I try Amsterdam because your parents had moved into a house there.'

I did not answer. I just pouted an invitation to be kissed.

'I just could not forget you,' explained Bob, 'so I applied for a post out here. It was not difficult, now we are in the Common Market.'

At that moment, Uncle Jan emerged from the tavern and staggered drunkenly over the bridge. 'That's it, little Riena, got a new boyfriend,' he slurred. 'I told you, there are plenty more fish in the sea.' He cackled loudly.

'Who the devil is that?' asked Bob.

'Oh, it is only my Uncle Jan,' I laughed. I was too happy to care and too busy to explain.

Riding High

I

For as long as I could remember, I had been in care. First it was in an orphange, then a series of foster homes. My brothers and sisters were all the other children, often unfortunates, in the homes and they were all kinds of creeds and colours. In spite of this start in life, I don't recall ever being unhappy. Luckily I had a sunny disposition. I was extraordinarily good-tempered and willing, and responded immediately to any affection.

I had never known my mother but I do know that she had given me a very sweet and English name. I was called Jasmine, after that lovely purple-leaved shrub which casts the sweet odours of its white flowers out in the evetide. I often imagined that I had been conceived in a swift passionate embrace under the jasmine in a hospital garden, for I knew that my mother was a nurse, an immigrant from Jamaica, and my father an Indian medical student.

That was all I knew about my background and I can't say that it was greatly appreciated by me. I resented the woolly hair that my mother had bequeathed to me, and the yellow skin that I had inherited from my Indian father.

At seven years old I was tall and boisterous, fit and healthy. Above all, I longed to be loved. And so when I was sent to a new foster home in the countryside I didn't mind. To me it was a new kind of adventure, and I was optimistic about finding what I wanted.

My white foster mother was lovely, calm and generous. She was also very religious. She lived in a village, in a pretty cottage, the front door of which opened straight into the living room. The house was always untidy but it had a warm, homely atmosphere. Although the floors were always scrubbed and the washing was snow white, Mum could never get around to dusting or putting things back where they belonged. As a result, the place was rather chaotic.

After a while, it became my task to restore law and order to the chaos. The strict, tidy discipline of the various institutions I had lived in made this an easy task for me and I enjoyed being able to make a difference to the place.

So Mum and I got on very well together, though I often offended her by removing the bow ribbon she would lovingly tie on my unruly hair. I would then spread it out neatly and re-tie it.

'Oh, you little fusspot,' she would say with a laugh.

My new dad was a very quiet man. When he was not at work he could always be found in the garden shed, puffing his smelly pipe, or sawing wood. Or he would be at his vegetable patch digging spuds. But he liked me. He was never too busy for a long cosy chat with me whenever I sought out his company. I was very fond of him.

Mum's life was very involved with the Church. She was a Roman Catholic and since there was no R.C. church in our small village, we had to take a trip to town on the bus to attend mass.

When the exciting decision was made that I was to live permanently with Mum and Dad, Mum took me from the village school and placed me at a very posh private convent school. Mum and Dad were only poor folk, so how they found the money for the school fees I shall never know. The daughters of the prosperous local farmers also attended the convent, as did anyone else who could afford to pay for this exclusive education.

So I, Jasmine, abandoned at birth, became the little lady. Soon I was speaking with my mouth full of peas and had my head stuffed with a lot of ideas on religion. Mum and Dad were extremely proud of me. And the school was good and remarkably tolerant. Until I was quite old, I was unaware of racial hatred or colour prejudice.

So for several years my life happily revolved around this nice school, the small country village and two loving, kind, and very indulgent parents.

Our tiny village, or hamlet, was tucked away amid dense woodland that swept down to the sea. All around there were acres and acres of rich farmland and miles of fruit orchards. And the small population knew each other's business very well indeed.

With my schoolfriends I went swimming in the river or riding on the heath. We felt as fresh and free as the lovely salt air. I loved riding and was a regular at the riding school from an early age. But it was at this riding school that my life changed.

The riding school was owned and run by an old man called Mr Fitch. He was bandy-legged, short-tempered, and very belligerent. But he was also a fine horseman. He lived only for his stables and the small plot of land he owned. He had turned fifty but was, so far, unmarried, and he was as lithe and nimble as a youth. And he liked me. I was good at handling the ponies and, with my straight back and long slim legs, I made a graceful rider. I quickly became Mr Fitch's favourite pupil.

When my parents had no money available for my riding lessons, Mr Fitch would allow me to work for it in the stables. I felt completely at home grooming the ponies' shiny backs, and whispering sweet nothings into those sensitive furry ears. In Mr Fitch's stables I was in my glory. The happiest days of my life were spent there, with Jingo, the old speckled mare, Peanut, Greensleeves and the many other mares and geldings that came and went. All were my friends and confidants.

Soon I had become the best horsewoman in the village. Mr Fitch trained me for the jumps, so I entered all the local events and took many prizes. For some reason I felt that I had not only to be good, but better than those rich girls with their smart outfits and expensive ponies which belonged to them.

It was at a local gymkhana that I had my first brush with colour prejudice. Before then it had never occurred to me that my colour could make any difference.

'Oh Mama,' cried a girl I had just beaten to second place on a matter of points. 'It's not fair, she shouldn't win, she's coloured.'

I listened to her mother's reply with horror.

'Yes, dear,' said her mother. 'This is supposed to be a local event. I'll see what I can do.'

Nothing happened to me. I still won the event but the clapping as Jingo and I did our lap of honour was muted. Back home at Mr Fitch's I told him what had happened.

Mr Fitch was furious. 'Damned woman!' he declared. 'You're the best little horsewoman in the district,' he shouted. 'I don't care if you're red, white or blue.'

But I had been deeply wounded, and made to feel like an outsider. From that time on, I became a little aloof. I spent more time with Jingo riding alone through the woodlands, trotting along the muddy leafy tracks, relishing the deep silence all around.

It was then that I got the idea that I wanted to own a horse of my own. I was fifteen and in my last year at school. Lately Dad had not been too well and Mum was very preoccupied looking after him, so I certainly could not ask for money. During the school holidays I went pea-picking and earned myself five pounds. Feeling very thrilled and optimistic I decided to ask Mr Fitch's advice about buying my own horse. We sat on a fallen oak tree watching a young foal and his mother as they pranced around the paddock.

Mr Fitch earned a fair living stabling and schooling mounts for the local farming gentry. He took off his checked cap and rubbed his grizzled grey head. 'Five pounds ain't much. You'd better save up a bit more,' he advised.

'No, I want my own horse now,' I said obstinately.

All that day I pestered poor old Mr Fitch to take me with him when he went to the monthly horse fair. Eventually, he looked at me rather ruefully. 'Trouble with women,' he grumbled, 'is that they won't give up once they've got the bit between their teeth. Just like horses, they are.'

'Oh, *please*, Mr Fitch,' I wheedled and cajoled him. 'I want so much to own my own horse. Jingo is lovely but you know she's getting past it.'

Mr Fitch had to agree with me about that. Suddenly he said; 'See that young mare in the paddock?'

'Sardi?' I asked.

He nodded. 'Got Arab blood in her, that one,' he remarked.

I gazed at the lovely bay scampering about the field with her chestnut foal.

'She's lively,' Mr Fitch said, 'but you could handle her. I'll see what I can do once the foal is weaned.'

Mr Fitch kept his promise. Sardi belonged to a very rich fruit farmer called Mr Wright who had bought her for his two daughters, Susan and Penny. Susan had married and gone to live abroad and the younger one, Penny, was fat and not a very good horsewoman. She had taken a bad fall last year and lost her nerve. That was why they had decided to breed from Sardi this year.

'For the cost of stabling and caring for the foal, the farmer might let the mare go cheap,' suggested Mr

Fitch. 'It will be more than five pounds, but I'll lend you the rest and then you can work for it.'

I was thrilled. Excitedly I informed Mum of my plan to become a professional horsewoman. She was kind but dubious. 'It costs a lot of money to keep a horse, dear.'

'Oh, I'll soon earn some money from competitions once I get a good horse,' I replied confidently. 'Don't worry about that.'

But I was sure she would and I looked into her pale, lined face. Mum worried over anything and everything.

My excellent plan developed a hitch. That fat simpleton, Penny Wright, insisted that she wanted to keep Sardi. The mare belonged to her and her sister, she said, even if she never rode again. And things were going to stay that way. Fortunately Penny's father was not so keen to keep a good mare just for pasture and neither was Mr Fitch. So after much argument, a plan was drawn up. I would care for and exercise Sardi until Penny made her mind up one way or the other.

I was not very pleased by this development. 'I want to buy a horse of my own,' I insisted, 'and I have five pounds to do so.'

Mr Wright almost laughed his head off when I came out with this but Mr Fitch was an astute businessman and a clever negotiator. 'Look,' he said, 'why not let Jasmine buy a share of Sardi? Penny will soon relent. We will train for the shows. Let Jasmine have a small share in Sardi and I'll raise the foal for you very cheaply,' he offered.

So in the end we reached an agreement. Sardi was valued at twenty pounds. Five of mine, five of Mr Fitch's and the farmer retained the other half.

It was a very amusing day. 'Well, that's settled,' laughed Mr Wright. 'We have all got one leg each. You take good care of my end.'

'It couldn't be in better hands,' Mr Fitch laughed back.

Later that day I was grooming Sardi's black mane and tail. The mare backed away and shook her head. I brushed her long neck and whispered words of comfort in her ear. She settled down as though she knew that we would become close friends.

Looking back now, that summer was glorious. It was a year I shall always remember. I may only have owned one leg of Sardi, but I felt that morally she was mine. Carefully I looked after her, groomed, fed and exercised her. We became almost inseparable. She was a very lively little mare with a will of her own, but under my hands she was gentle and willing, nimble and clever. No words can describe my love of that first horse.

On my next birthday, my parents and Mr Fitch got together and bought me a complete set of new riding clothes: a tweed waisted jacket, light breeches, high leather boots, a black velvet riding hat, and a little crop, that I never used.

At school I felt happy and secure. I sat for my O levels and passed in chemistry and physics. Then I had the whole summer to spend with Sardi. Mr Fitch had bought a new horse-box which he hitched up to his jeep. In this we travelled around the country at weekends entering the one-day events. Sardi was great. She won many prizes and well earned her keep, while I obtained a skill and sense of my own ability.

During the week we taught a string of children to ride. There were plenty of youngsters wanting to learn. The population of the little hamlet was growing rapidly as new bungalows sprang up around the area like mushrooms. The character of our hamlet was changing, too.

'Crowding us in,' Mr Fitch remarked somewhat sadly, though he was not sorry to get the extra business.

Every evening during that summer holiday we rode over the heath with our pony train of children dressed up in their posh outfits. The money Mr Fitch made from these wealthy enthusiasts was always invested in our outings to shows, events and gymkhanas.

Around the time we were expecting Farmer Wright to sell his half of Sardi to us – for Penny had lost all interest in her – we received an extremely unpleasant shock. A large youth with freckles and a mop of red hair arrived at the stables one day. He announced that he was called Erwin and he was Farmer Wright's nephew and the new owner of Sardi's other half. Mr Wright, it seemed, had sold his shares in the horse to his nephew.

I was astonished and furious. How could this happen? How *dare* Farmer Wright do such a thing when he knew how much Sardi meant to me! Mr Fitch, always the diplomat, remained calm and unmoved. Placing a restraining hand on my arm, he turned to the lad. 'You *can* ride, I suppose,' he said.

'No,' said the youth. 'I want to learn. We've just moved in from town.'

'A townie,' I sneered. 'Teaching *you* is going to take a bit of doing.'

Erwin's bright blue eyes looked back at me with a hurt expression. 'Well,' he muttered quietly, 'if it's going to cause too much trouble, I'll ask my uncle to call off the deal.'

Now Mr Fitch was, in all things, a businessman, and Farmer Wright brought a lot of business his way. 'Now, now, there's no problem,' he said in a pleasant voice. 'We can work this out. Now, you can't learn to ride on Sardi, for she's too temperamental, but you can go out with Jasmine on Jingo until you are riding confidently. Then we'll talk shop.'

So for two evenings each week, when I should have been practising my showjumping, I had to teach this ridiculous boy to ride. He seemed much younger than I, but he was, in fact, two months older. He was also very awkward and somewhat overweight. He fell off Jingo many times (and I usually grinned with pleasure when he did), but he made no fuss at all. In fact, he was always remarkably jolly and good-tempered.

To my surprise, I realized that after a while I began to look forward to these jaunts with Erwin along the forest tracks. I had never had a close chum before, unless you could count Mr Fitch, and I enjoyed the experience. Gradually we became fast friends. As his riding improved, I was more willing to let him have a go on Sardi. But the first time he got on her she bucked and threw him, four miles from home and bolted off, so we both had to ride back to the stables on Jingo. Having Erwin's arms looped about my waist was a warm, pleasant feeling. When we got back, there was Sardi, her reins around her fetlocks, looking very pleased with herself.

Erwin was an extraordinarily happy and easy-going boy. That summer he turned seventeen, and passed his driving test. He was a good driver and could handle Mr Fitch's old jeep very well. Now he began to accompany us on our outings to the one-day events and share the driving with Mr Fitch. We often sang merrily on the way home, and we were never depressed regardless of whether I had won or not. It was just fun being in such good company.

When the sharp winds of autumn stole over the heath, Erwin and I parted. He went away to do a course at an agricultural college, while I, having left school, started my studies as a physiotherapist. The course required two days of voluntary work at the local hospital in town.

Erwin and I wrote regularly to each other during this period. We were pals with the same interest at heart. I was aware that new feelings for Erwin were stirring in my body. Whilst at my studies, I often dreamed of his auburn hair and his ready smile. And I knew that the flickerings of love were already in my heart.

Early in the spring, I rode Sardi along the forest tracks. The winter had been long, cold and hard. Sardi, lacking exercise, was extremely frisky. The air was cold and crisp, but the countryside was very pretty. The hedgerows were pushing out their green buds and yellow clumps of primroses dotted the woodland path. I felt conscious and proud of my well-groomed appearance. I had my riding clothes on and, having allowed my hair to grow longer, it was neatly tied up in a fine hair-net under my riding hat.

My thoughts were, as usual, on Erwin. He would be home at Easter. It will be nice to have company to ride with in the woods once more, I thought. Little tugs of excitement stirred inside me each time I thought about him.

Suddenly Sardi leaped in the air and let out a little buck. 'Whoa, there, Sardi!' I cried as she kicked out her back legs. 'Has the spring got into you, too?'

Erwin arrived one sunny Sunday morning as Mr Fitch and I were cleaning out the stables. I was dressed in an old pair of overalls and smelled heavily of manure. But this did not put off Erwin. He came over and gave me a great bear hug. 'Oh, it's great to see you again, Jasmine,' he almost bellowed.

I was embarrassed and could feel a blush creeping across my face. Erwin was looking very handsome. He had filled out and was by no means fat any longer. The months of absence had really altered him; he was a mature young man. As soon as I had recovered from my shyness, I began to show him my skill at the fences with Sardi.

Later we sat drinking coffee in Mr Fitch's parlour beside the mantelpiece and sideboard, which were covered with cups and trophies that I had won. On the wall, hundreds of rosettes were hanging – bright ribbons of red, blue, yellow, or green, depending on where I had been placed in that competition. Together the three of us planned future events and then, to my amazement, I managed to persuade both Mr Fitch and Erwin to sell their shares in Sardi. Erwin had decided that he would rather buy a bigger horse that could carry his weight and accommodate his long legs without any trouble.

'You need one at least sixteen hands high,' said Mr Fitch. 'I'll see what I can do.' He puffed his pipe and looked at us thoughtfully as I cuddled close to Erwin. I was radiating happiness, so pleased I was that Sardi was to be mine at last.

Well, it was inevitable that Erwin's and my friendship should develop into something more – a real love affair, in fact. First the petting started and then we got more and more involved. On our rides to the woodlands with Jingo and Sardi, the horses would quietly munch the green grass as Erwin and I made love. Gradually we became hopelessly and helplessly infatuated with each other.

I had never been to Erwin's home or met his parents, but I knew where he lived and had often gazed with curiosity at that lovely detached bungalow with its well-laid-out gardens as I passed by on horseback. I knew nothing of Erwin's family life. All I knew was that he was Penny Wright's cousin. I had been at school with her and she had never liked me, but that was long ago and it never occurred to me that there was any real reason for anyone to dislike me.

In the early summer, the round of weekend gymkhanas began again. Sardi was on better form than ever and started winning straight away. Erwin had become a real horse lover, and since he had started at agricultural college, had decided to breed horses.

'I'm a farmer first and foremost, Jasmine,' he said, 'but when we marry and get a place of our own, I'd like to breed good thoroughbreds. There's money in it.' I knew that running a stud was an expensive business, but Erwin's optimism and belief in his abilities really enchanted me. I was happy and content. There seemed to be no cloud on my horizon.

It was my mother who tried to warn me to be cautious. 'Darling,' she said, 'don't get too involved with Erwin. It might bring you trouble.'

'Trouble?' I said, eyebrows raised in scorn. Mum was such a worrier.

'I know his mother,' my mother continued. 'She has a hairdressing salon in town and she's a real dragon. I did some housework for her once, but never again.'

Since Dad had been forced to give up work because of ill-health, Mum had taken to doing housework around the village. I was a little resentful that she was now a home-help. I had got myself a student grant and begged her to let up, but so far she had not. I loved her dearly, but I could not confide in her about how deeply involved with Erwin I was. She was so deeply religious and her faith always maintained that one should remain pure before marriage. I could not help it but my nature was hot and passionate. I was frantically in love, so I replied rather rudely, 'I'm not concerned with his mother. This has got nothing to do with her.'

My mother sighed. 'Oh well, dear,' she said resignedly, 'don't say I didn't warn you.'

I still did my two days' voluntary work as part of my training. During these days I took disabled children swimming and helped out in the heat-treatment clinic. Erwin often met me afterwards, and we would have a meal out or go to the pictures.

One night he was particularly jubilant. 'I've just taken my folks to the airport,' he grinned. 'They've gone to Spain until September.' This was the first time he had ever mentioned his parents. 'Now we've got the house to ourselves, so we'll have a whale of a time.' And indeed we did . . .

That summer I spent most of my off-duty hours, when I wasn't at the stables, in this pleasant bungalow with its secluded gardens. Erwin and I were as wrapped up with each other as two people can be. I did not spend the night there, of course, because of my parents, but I did spent a lot of time in Erwin's parents' double bed.

Erwin had bought himself a four-year-old colt, a big rangy-looking animal that suited his height. His name was Toffy and we soon began to train him for show-jumping. Sometimes we entered both him and Sardi for the one-day events with me as the rider, and whenever I rode to victory, I felt my head was in the clouds. My fantasies revolved around ideas of international show events, and of my becoming Horsewoman of the Year.

The local folk muttered and twittered about our behaviour, but we didn't care. We lived for every happy moment. On my birthday, Erwin bought me a ring. It was a small sapphire surrounded with diamonds. 'When my parents come home I'm going to tell them I want to get married,' he said. 'In fact, I might even write and tell them ahead,' he added a little nervously.

On Saturday evenings, we often joined Mr Fitch at the local pub and sometimes Erwin's friends from the local cricket club joined us. I shall never forget that fateful night in the tavern soon after Erwin had given me the ring. I had dressed up to go out that evening for a change. Usually I wore old jeans and a sweater but that night I had chosen a low-necked pink jumper and a long black skirt. I had had my hair done at the hairdresser's, so that it was soft, black and shiny.

'You look fabulous,' said Erwin, appreciatively, 'you should always dress like that.' We sat close together with a circle of friends. One girl in particular, Julie, had a terrific sense of humour and we laughed at her jokes until we cried. 'Hey,' Julie suddenly said, giving Erwin a nudge with her elbow. 'Just look at who has walked in.'

A middle-aged couple were standing at the bar. Both were very tanned and rather prosperous looking. The woman wore a smart silver-grey dress which almost matched her silvery blonde hair. She was very slim and looked tiny next to her husband, who was big and fat and wore large glasses. Immediately I knew that they were Erwin's parents.

Sheepishly Erwin got up and walked over to them. At the bar they all had a long discussion, and at one point I saw Erwin's father patting his son on the back in a cajoling manner. I turned my head slightly and my gaze met two dark eyes staring back at me from under that white lacquered hair. The look in those eyes expressed nothing but pure dislike.

I shuddered as if a ghost had walked over my grave. To avoid further embarrassment, I got up and, trying to look nonchalant, put some money in the jukebox and selected a couple of tunes. I could feel my cheeks burning. A wave of loud music suddenly drowned my thoughts. I was relieved. Turning round again, I saw that Erwin and his parents had left the bar. I didn't need to be told that Erwin's mother had refused to meet me.

When I returned to our table, there was a strained atmosphere among our friends. Everyone had witnessed this scene. Although nothing had been said, they all knew what had happened. I sat in silence, cradling my drink and trying not to let the tears well up in my eyes.

Half an hour later, Erwin returned. He looked quite pale and shaken. 'I wasn't expecting them back until next month,' he muttered. 'I'm afraid that's the end of our playing house.'

So, for the first Saturday evening that summer, I was home at ten o'clock. Mum and Dad made no comment, but they were unusually kind to me.

The next week when Erwin and I met, it was hell. Erwin looked so anxious and depressed, and sometimes it looked as if he had been crying. I asked no questions. I just held him close, vowing that nothing and nobody would come between us.

In spite of my show of bravado I was really concerned about what was happening. My mother picked this up immediately. 'Darling,' she said in that calm, loving manner, Erwin's mother will never let him marry you. You must accept that. Just be sensible and look about for someone else.'

Her blunt words shocked me. 'But why?' I demanded. 'Am I such a terrible person? And she doesn't even know me.'

Mum held my hand in her rough ones and said gently: 'No, dear. You are loving, beautiful and loyal. In fact, you are everything a man could ever wish for.'

'Well, why won't she even bother to get to know me?' I complained bitterly.

Mum sighed. 'It's just that there are a lot of folk like that in this world, dear. And there is little we can do about it,' she said.

I knew what she was hinting at. 'Because I'm coloured, is that what you mean?' I asked. It was more of a statement than a question.

'Please, darling, don't get hurt. There's a hard cold world out there waiting for you and you've been brought up in a very sheltered spot. You're like a little black lamb in a field of white sheep. It won't be so important later on when you've decided your future, but you are vulnerable until then,' explained Mum.

Now a big hurt had opened up inside me. 'I'll never believe that my colour matters to Erwin until he tells me himself,' I declared obstinately.

But then Erwin began to miss our arranged meetings, often sending messages to say that he was too busy working on his uncle's farm helping with the harvest. Mr Fitch and I exercised Sardi and Toffy, and went off to one-day events on our own. But the spirit had gone from my riding.

To cheer me up, Mr Fitch took me to the horse fair one day. We had a grand time watching those beautiful thoroughbreds in the ring and listening to the noise and clatter in the beer tent where men did private deals and talked of nothing but horse flesh.

One evening I returned from my hospital job and right away I knew that Mum had had a visitor earlier that day. The best china teapot and cups were on a tray in the front room. These were a giveaway since we lived most of our time in the warm back kitchen. Dad was sitting beside the kitchen range, a bronchial cough racking his lungs, while Mum seemed rather harassed. Two bright spots of temper shone on her usually pallid cheeks.

'She's been here,' I said immediately.

'Yes, dear,' replied Mum. 'I'm afraid it has not been a very pleasant afternoon. Erwin's mother is a very neurotic woman. I pray to God that you never do have her for a mother-in-law.'

'Oh, she must be mad coming here,' I said. 'Don't let her upset you, she doesn't bother me.' I tried desperately to console Mum. I felt that I had to speak to Erwin. I was so churned up inside that I did not know what else I could do. I rang his uncle, Farmer Wright, at the farm and eventually got hold of Erwin.

He sounded rather distant and cagey. 'I can't see you now, Jasmine,' he said. 'Mother's ill. I'll come

Sunday morning.' But before that time the climax had been reached.

Erwin's mother had taken an overdose. The receptionist at the hospital was from our village and she rang me at the office of the physiotherapy clinic. 'They just brought in your future mother-in-law, Jasmine,' she said. 'Sleeping pills,' she added with what I detected as malicious candour.

Unable to contain my curiosity, I almost ran to reception just in time to see Erwin's mother being pushed down the corridor. She lay on a stretcher, her mouth wide open, her false teeth removed, her blonde hair awry and the pallor of death upon her face. She looked a dreadful sight.

Walking beside her was Erwin, his hands pressed to his eyes. He was too distraught even to recognize me.

I waited anxiously for news as the doctors fought for her life. I could not bring myself to approach Erwin. It seemed like such a personal matter, much as I wanted to comfort him. A nagging uneasy feeling came over me. Had I been the cause of his mother attempting suicide? And deep down I knew that I had.

Erwin spent all day and nearly all night at his mother's bedside until his father came to take him home. Once his mother was out of danger, I waited patiently for him to contact me. But again, in my innermost heart I knew that he would not. I knew that it was all over.

On one of the many sleepless nights that followed, as I tossed and turned in bed, I made my decision. My mother's words had been haunting me all day: 'a little black lamb in a field of white sheep'. And I knew that

I had to get away from the shelter. I had to get out into the world. I knew that Erwin's parents were rejecting me solely for my skin colour. And now Erwin was too. Up until now I had chosen to ignore the difference between me and everyone else in the village. I had chosen to believe that it made no difference. And it did not make a difference to me – it was *others* who cared about skin pigmentation. But I was so anxious about it now. I thought about other coloured people I knew – not very many at all. There were black girls working at the hospital. They all seemed quite happy and well-adjusted with black and white people alike. But I didn't associate with them as a rule. In fact, I generally acted as if I were white. Perhaps that irritated people. Certainly it could not be sensible of me to do this. I had to face up to reality now – the little black lamb has got to lift its head up high and look at the world straight in the eye.

Erwin arrived at the stables on Sunday morning when I was schooling Sardi in the paddock. He looked pale and rather distraught. Without conversing, I waited while he saddled his horse and then we rode out together into the forest. It was late autumn and those lovely rusty tints were on the leaves of the beech trees. The air was crisp and cold as we galloped over the soft moist ground. Halting at our usual spot under a great oak that spread its branches like an umbrella over a green glade, we sat on a bed of ferns where we had often made love in the past.

Erwin had been preoccupied all the way there. Now he said in a quiet voice, 'It's over, Jasmine, dear.

Forgive me but I cannot go on.' His large fair freckled hands clutched at the riding whip until the knuckles showed white.

I suppose I should have been sensible and accepted his surrender but I was not. Instead, I threw my arms about his neck. 'Please don't leave me, darling,' I cried. 'Let's run off somewhere away from this place, where no one will know us.'

I could feel Erwin shaking his head. Firmly he removed my arms from his neck. I felt desperate and agitated. 'Just let's make love once more,' I pleaded. I was convinced that once we embraced Erwin would change his mind.

But he stared at me, horrified. Pulling away from me, he got to his feet, leaped on Toffy and rode away. I watched the horse's chestnut flanks shining in the weak autumnal sun and its long tail swishing as my lover rode away out of my life.

Sardi ambled over to where I was sitting and nuzzled me gently. I put my arms about her neck and wept heartbroken tears into her silky coat. She grunted and pushed me gently with her soft nose as if she understood how I was feeling.

That evening I wrote two letters. One was to my foster parents asking them to forgive me for what I was about to do, and the other was to Mr Fitch begging him to take care of Sardi until I had earned enough money to be able to take her and look after her myself.

At dawn the next day, I crept down the stairs and caught the first bus into town. By seven o'clock I was speeding on my way to the big city. I didn't know where

I was bound but I knew that I had to experience the world and find my true self. The one certainty was that I could no longer live in that sheltered country village.

II

London, the swinging city. So this was it. I was in a state of shock. In fact, I had never been so confused and distressed before. I wandered around the metropolis seeking a sanctuary from this horrifying world of noise, hustle, bustle and crowds of unfriendly people.

I arrived at Victoria Station just as the first batch of workers commuted in. It was the middle of the rush hour. They burst out of the trains and dashed towards the barriers, all bearing the same grim expression on their faces. No one offered to help as I struggled along with my heavy suitcase.

Once outside the station the noise of the traffic seemed deafening. I had never heard anything like it. Then a police car dashed past with its blue light flashing and siren screaming. This was followed by an even noisier fire engine. In bewilderment, I stopped in my tracks, anchored to the spot.

A shifty-looking youth edged up close to me. He had long tousled hair and wore a grubby red sweater. 'You wanna taxi?' he asked.

Nervously, I stepped away from him, shook my head and moved on, lugging my heavy case for several blocks as I looked for signs of accommodation. I had a little money with me, but even I knew that it would not go very far in those brightly lit hotels. So I made my way towards the meaner streets, occasionally stopping to put my case down to relieve my aching arm.

Now I saw a bed and breakfast sign. This was more like it. Climbing the front steps, I rang the bell of that sleazy house. Within moments a blowsy woman had opened the door. She looked me up and down and said abruptly; 'No vacancies!' Then she slammed the door in my face.

She was the first of many. This kind of thing went on all day until, eventually, I found myself back outside Victoria Station. I had completed the circle.

The same shifty-looking youth was there. His familiarity made him seem friendly to me, and his voice was certainly not hostile. 'Cor blimey,' he exclaimed. 'Ain't you got fixed up yet?'

With tear-filled eyes I shook my head.

'Well,' he said – I had trouble following what he said, his accent was so odd – 'get rid of that blooming suitcase for a start.'

'Get rid of it?' I stared at him in puzzlement.

'Put it in the Left Luggage.' He jerked his thumb in the direction of the station. 'No one'll pick it out of there.'

Instantly, I knew that this was sound advice. I followed him to the Left Luggage Office and put my suitcase away. Now I looked at my new companion more closely. He was still wearing his grubby red jersey and his hair was very untidy. I looked at him a little distastefully. But he did have kind eyes, I thought.

The boy was undeterred by my scrutiny. 'Let's get a cup of coffee,' he suggested. 'Then I'll show you where to find some digs.'

He was very friendly and obliging, so I followed him into a small café which smelled overpoweringly of onions.

'Right,' the boy said, rubbing his dirty hands together in anticipation, and staring hungrily at the food in a glass display case. I suddenly realized that he was waiting for me to order. 'Two coffees,' I said. 'I'm not hungry, but you have what you want. I'll pay.'

Without hesitation or thanks, he ordered two revolting-looking sausage rolls. We found a table and sat down opposite each other. He sat busily munching those greasy rolls with much enjoyment. I was so glad just to rest my feet that I remained silent, just enjoying my first opportunity to relax since my arrival in London.

When he had finished eating, the boy wiped the back of his hand across his lips. 'Now,' he said, 'to work. You got much money?' He eyed my handbag greedily.

I placed a protective hand over it. 'Not much,' I replied. 'Just enough until I get some work.'

'Work?' He looked stunned for a second and then he said, 'Go rahnd Social Security termorrer. Yer can get a couple of quid to tide yer over.'

I was not exactly sure what he meant, but I said sharply, 'Well now, tell me where I can get clean, cheap lodgings.'

The boy grinned and ignored my request. 'Me name's Pokey,' he said cordially.

'Pokey?' I repeated in amusement.

'Yus, funny, ain't it?' he said. 'I got that nickname

'cos I always had me finger stuck up me nose when I was a kid.'

'How disgusting!' I murmured.

''Ere,' he said, 'you're a bit toffee-nosed for a darkie, ain't yer?'

I frowned and got to my feet. I was quite offended. No one had ever spoken to me like that before. 'I'd better go,' I said quickly. 'It's getting dark.'

Pokey grinned. 'All right, don't lose yer shirt,' he said. 'I'll go wiv yer to show yer where the hostel is. You'll be all right there tonight.'

The place, as Pokey described it, sounded reasonable, so I was happy to follow him through a maze of back streets, walking a little way behind his shambling figure until we came to a tall, gloomy house.

'In there,' Pokey said, 'but I'm orf. I don't want to let them see you wiv me.' With that, he scampered away.

As I entered the house, a feeling of deep depression sank into my chest. To the left was a large reception room. It was full of people sitting or lounging around on the sofas, chairs and even the floor. They were mostly girls, women and even very small children all waiting to be bedded down for the night.

Polite, smiling social workers moved in among them, taking notes and then guiding them in various directions. They did seem to resemble a herd of sheep, only, unlike the white herd my mother had referred to, this one was made up of all colours – black, brown, white and yellow. But these were all human beings, all homeless and desolate like me. But not like me. I was *not* like them. I wanted to turn and run away from this scene but I was too terrified of the dark city outside. I sat in a chair and I waited my turn to answer their questions. Yes, I was homeless. I had just arrived. I had no home (that lie made me feel very guilty), and hardly any money.

'Nothing to worry about, dear,' said the social workers. 'We'll give you bed and breakfast, and then we'll see about getting you other accommodation in the morning.' The kindness of the people who worked in this hostel really touched me. I wasn't sure if I felt like an imposter or not.

I spent that long night sitting up, too afraid was I to lie down in those rough although clean sheets. All around me the women snored or talked in their sleep, and one old lady went back and forth to the toilet nearly all night. Nevertheless, I was glad to be safe from the terrors outside.

In the morning I washed at a long line of sinks with a thick towel and disinfectant soap. Many of the women larked about as if the morning light had lifted their spirits. Some sang and even danced, their bare breasts swinging. But others just stared gloomily out of pale, unhealthy faces.

Downstairs, over cornflakes and a boiled egg, I sat silently at table. No one seemed concerned or even interested in me. At one point a girl asked if I smoked. 'I'm dying for a fag,' she said. I shook my head and she lost interest as someone else provided her with a cigarette.

At eleven o'clock, I sat in the social worker's office while she made a series of phone calls. 'Yes, yes, nice, clean, bright girl. She's just arrived. Yes, half-and-half, I believe.'

I knew immediately that she was referring to my coffee-coloured skin and my posh accent. Clearly, she thought I was half-white, but I could not tell if this was better than being wholly black, or all the same. It was confusing.

Eventually I was installed in lodgings and given a green card to obtain a job in a coffee bar, which I did. My room was right at the top of a house owned by a very nice, although noisy, Jamaican family. It was a very bare room, but I didn't mind about that. I just wanted to be alone with my broken heart.

The job was vile but I knew I had to stick at it as I was desperate for the money. There was an endless stream of cups of tea and coffee to be poured, and I hated the hot, stifling atmosphere and the rude, irritable customers. They all contributed towards a gradually growing inner feeling of discontentment.

For my hard work, I earned twenty pounds per week and had a midday meal. I paid eight pounds a week for my sky-high room, so all told I wasn't too badly off.

Before long, my social life began to brighten up. The Jamaicans were seldom home during the week – they were either out working or visiting. But at weekends when they were at home, life in the house became extremely lively. Friends and relations came round for wonderfully rowdy parties. And all the tenants joined in.

My downstairs neighbour was a white girl called Mollie who lived with a dark-skinned man. Every night she donned a black wig, painted her skin darker and went off to work. Because of that, she slept all day. It was very strange to me, and I found that I was rather curious about her. Then at one of those lively house-parties we became friends. Mollie was a lively girl from Tyneside. She had short, cropped hair, wore see-through saris and little else. 'I'm a belly-dancer, love,' she informed me. 'You know, I wiggles and woggles.' She wobbled her belly and went off into peals of laughter.

Now dancing was something I did know about, having received excellent tuition in tap and ballet at my posh school. 'Is it hard to do?' I asked.

'No, love, it's easy. All you have to do is adopt your own style. If you make it a bit sexy, you get well paid. Can you dance?' she asked.

'A little,' I replied.

'You've got a smashing figure,' she said. 'Some of them strip clubs like light-coloured types.'

I stared at her. 'You mean you take all your clothes off?' I was as shocked as I sounded.

'Yeah, so what?' said the irrepressible Mollie. 'They're always trying to strip you, so you might just as well be paid for it.'

I wasn't quite sure what she was talking about but I considered this conversation very carefully.

Before long, I was doing the rounds with Mollie, dashing from club to club in a taxi. Mollie worked hard, putting on four shows in one night, doing battle with strippers and showgirls. Thus, this cheerful exuberant Geordie earned her way by wiggling her beautiful body for hours. She could earn fifty pounds in one night.

These late nights caught up with me, and in no time I was dismissed from my coffee-pouring job because I was incapable of getting up in time in the mornings after my night out on the town with Mollie. By this time, the obvious thing to do seemed to be to join my friend, so I did.

Mollie taught me the rudimentary movements of belly-dancing and lent me a costume. Then I got an engagement in a Turkish club.

'Stick it for a while, love,' Mollie advised me. 'Then later you can change and freelance like me. Don't let the blokes worry you. Just do your job, pick up your lolly and get back home to sleep. Like that, you'll survive.'

At first I performed a kind of classic ballet that I'd learned at school, but soon discovered how to hot up the act, and to wear less. After a few weeks I changed my name to Yasmin, claiming that I was of Turkish extraction. I oiled my hair so that it hung fairly straight, and wore long false eyelashes that veiled my eyes. I took no notice of the dark sensuous faces about me, just drew my pay and put it in the bank. I felt very detached from what I was doing. And I knew that I was becoming hardened and bitter.

I had never got used to the big city. Always within me was a keen longing for the cool green forest and the feel of Sardi's warm flanks between my legs. Alone in my bed in my attic room, I still dreamed of being a professional horsewoman with a string of thoroughbreds.

After a while, I went home to visit my parents and Mr Fitch for the occasional weekend. I lied about what I was doing in the capital but my parents were so relieved that I had got back in touch and appeared not to have come to any apparent harm that they asked no difficult questions. They would have died if they had learned the truth about my life at that point, and I felt guilty about deceiving them. But I had no choice if I wanted to see them again.

I pretended that I was very happy with my new life, that city living was just what I had craved for. But the truth was that I had by no means found peace and contentment in that multi-racial society. I had grown afraid of the boisterous Jamaicans at the clubs who wanted to date me. I disliked the slimy married men, who came to gloat over my almost naked body, and every night I still dreamed of Erwin with his fresh complexion and ready smile. But I could not tell my mother any of this. So I lied and told her that all was well.

One day I received a letter from Mr Fitch written in his neat, old-fashioned hand. He wrote to tell me that the pending motorway extension was now going to pass through our lovely woodland. He was most unhappy about it, but the council had compensated him well. With the money he had purchased another place not far from London and his greatest wish was that I should visit him there. Jingo, Peanut and Sardi were all still with him.

Oh, how happy I was that Sunday morning when I stepped off the train and saw Mr Fitch outside the station in that familiar old jeep. He looked older, his face was more lined, but he was as jolly and hearty as ever. He now lived in a nice modern bungalow with a large paddock and plenty of grazing land. The horses recognized me immediately, each one pushing its head forward to be fussed. I wept tears of joy as I saw my old saddle in the tackroom, carefully cleaned and saddle-soaped, just waiting for me.

'Don't suppose you do much riding in that old town,' said Mr Fitch with a chuckle. 'We'll have a quick lunch and then ride out over the weald. There's some beautiful country about here.'

In the paddock after lunch, Mr Fitch saddled a chestnut youngster. 'Recognize her?' he asked mysteriously.

'Why, it's Sara Sue, Sardi's foal!' I cried with delight.

Mr Fitch gently stroked her long neck. 'She's three now. I've got great hopes for her,' he said dreamily.

That afternoon I was back riding Sardi, with Mr Fitch on Sara Sue. Oh, what joy that was! The feel of the horse between my legs, the warm sun, the exquisite, quiet, green countryside . . . these were all the things that made me happy.

It was the first of many Sundays spent with Mr Fitch. For me, Saturday was a very busy night but I was never too tired to catch that midday train down to Silver Birches, as Mr Fitch had named his place.

By the middle of the summer I was back in action, entering the mid-week events, winning prizes and gaining prestige all round. Sardi and I still made a good team.

One afternoon, Mr Fitch and I sat beside a log fire.

It was a cool day, almost autumnal, and our tea and toast was going down very well after our brisk ride.

'Exactly what do you do at this job in town?' asked Mr Fitch, lighting up his pipe.

'Belly-dancing,' I replied with a grin. Suddenly I was amused by how I earned my living.

Mr Fitch nodded and sucked on his pipe. 'Oh, the ballet, very nice,' he commented. 'Very elegant.'

Oh, well, I thought, he's missed his chance to know and I was not going to give him another one.

'I know you make good money,' he said, 'but it's not everything dear,' he said thoughtfully. 'Would you consider giving it up to stay here with me and train Sara Sue? Then you can enter her for events next year as well as Sardi?'

This suggestion came at a time when I was so uncertain about my life and the direction it was taking, yet I felt that, now that I had tasted a bit of life outside the confined village I had grown up in, I was more capable of making a firm, rational decision. As Mr Fitch continued to tell me his plans, I could feel a mounting excitement inside me.

'I'll not part with Jingo,' he was saying. 'I've had her too long and, like me, she's getting past it. But I intend to build this place up, not as a riding school, but as a breeding farm for three-day eventers.'

'That's very exciting,' I cried, 'but surely it'll cost the earth to establish.'

'The money's not a problem,' Mr Fitch said. 'I've got enough put aside. What I need is reliable, experienced assistance. I've got to have someone good. And you're perfect, Jasmine. Come and stay here, you'll be a great asset to me if you do. We could really work hard together and make a success of the place.'

'Oh, Mr Fitch!' I rushed at him and hugged him impulsively. 'Do you really mean it?' I felt as though all my life's problems, all dilemmas about the future, were solved.

''Course I do,' he retorted. 'I'd be wasting my breath otherwise.'

I thought of the store of money that I'd earned. 'I'll buy a good brood mare of my own. I've got money saved,' I declared jubilantly.

'And we'll have to get ourselves the best stallion we can find.'

Mr Fitch held out his gnarled hand. 'It's a deal. Shake on it, partner,' he cried.

I clutched those bony fingers, my life line, and shook them hard. I had never been happier.

My mother didn't approve of these plans at first. 'People will talk,' she wrote. 'Why not come home now? Certain people you don't wish to meet have left the village and gone to Canada . . .'

I knew that she meant Erwin and his family and I was annoyed by her coyness. 'Nuts!' I said impatiently as I tore up that letter.

So began my new love affair. There were no men in my life, only horses. And I was more contented than I'd ever been. Together Mr Fitch and I built up a string of three-day eventers. Within two years we were well known across the country, horsemen and women came to us for schooling from all over Kent.

This year, I won a major national three-day event on Sara Sue. I hope to do even better next year. And now I am running the place on my own.

Sadly, my dear friend Mr Fitch passed away one winter's day. 'Pick up the reins when I drop them, Jasmine,' he had said enigmatically one evening as we sat down after supper. He peacefully went off to sleep in his chair, never to wake up again.

I felt so desolate without him, but that beloved little man is still always here. His spirit hovers protectively around the house and in the stable. And whenever I kiss old Jingo he is beside me. He left everything to me in his will – his house and shares in the stables. My parents have moved here now, so we are all together again. So once more I am riding high.

Will I marry? Yes, I think so, one day. But my main purpose then will be to raise children in a happy home, to give them the love and security I did not get from my own parents but was lucky to have from my foster parents. I know that in spite of the identity crisis that sent me off to London, my foster parents had given me a good grounding for life so that when presented with what I needed in life, I was confident enough to know it and to take it.

The Willows Wept with Me

'Five tall elm trees in a straight line, A garden where honeysuckle and wild rose entwine . . .'

As I pedal my bicycle through the country lanes, I often chant these lines aloud. They always remind me of a special spot down by the Thames, a spot that was both my haven of past happiness and a place of great sorrow. It is an image that I can never erase from my mind.

Today is my day off and, as always, summer or winter, I am making the same trip down to the river, to an open space bordered by a line of impressive elms, as in the rhyme. It is a wild, overgrown spot by a broken-down slipway, next to which lies a derelict boat that has remained there for at least the past ten years, and probably more.

Since I started coming here again, the only changes are that the elms are taller, the foliage wilder, more overgrown, and the boat even more pathetic, with rotten planks occasionally falling from the mooring and floating down the river. I don't care about the growing decay. This is *my* spot, my solitary haven. It is here that I dwell on thoughts about my love, and sometimes I imagine that I can see his face in the dark, deep river water. For this is where he went to his death, carried out by the merciless tide, never to be found again.

An uncontrollable force compels me to return here time and time again. I often try to stop myself even as I prepare to set off on the journey. 'Don't go, Jenny,' I say to myself, 'it does no good, he will not return.' But I cannot stop myself. The desire to be here is stronger than my reason. Not once have I actually not set off to ride the ten miles from the country home for disabled children where I am assistant matron, to the place where I can commune with the happy times and my love.

Now as I ride on my bike towards my destination, my mind immediately turns to Raymond. Yet again, I can see him, hobbling down from his hut to the river to attend to his fishing line. Tears come to my eyes as I relieve the past, allowing the memories to sweep over me once again.

My story begins when I left Ireland at the age of fourteen. I came to London during the war and worked hard to become a nurse in a London teaching hospital. I was good at my studies and was lucky, in a sense, because my plain appearance meant that I did not have the distractions more attractive girls had, with their boyfriends and exciting, time-consuming dates. I was – and still am – small and dumpy, short-sighted and mousy. I did not have a boyfriend until I was eighteen.

It was just after the war when I met Ray, at a time when I was feeling settled and content with my life and work. It hadn't been easy to study and cope with the extra work during the London Blitz, but pride in and love for my job had enabled me to come through with a kind of inner peace which compensated for my lack of a social life.

It was his name which caught my eye in the medical reports of the new patient in Men's Medical Ward: Raymond Beharrel. What a nice name, I thought. It seemed to roll off the tongue.

I went on to read his medical file. He had won a brave fight for survival after suffering appalling injuries from a shell while serving in the Desert Army. He had lost both his legs as well as an eye in the terrible burns to his face. He was here in the hospital for skin grafting on one side of his disfigured face.

When first I met him, Raymond was propped up in bed with his face heavily bandaged. He immediately winked at me with his good eye, this young man of twenty-two. Nursing makes one hard, but that wink softened me instantly. I knew straight away that there was something special about this particular patient.

Raymond soon became everyone's favourite patient, I wasn't the only one to recognize his charms. He was so cheerful and good-natured in spite of what he had gone through and his disabilities. I enjoyed nursing him and had a special feeling for him when I just sat holding his hand in comfort as he cried out in pain or despondency after another visit to the operating theatre.

When he finally grew well enough, I wheeled

Raymond around the hospital grounds, talking to him, and trying not to let him feel self-conscious about the scarred side of his face. And my heart would jump whenever he turned and grinned that winning way at me.

Almost unconsciously, Raymond and I grew very close until a time when it seemed perfectly natural for me to kiss him gently on the forehead, to hug him and kiss him on the lips with encouragement when he started to try to walk with the artificial legs with which he had been fitted.

However, before long, he had to leave to go to an artificial limbs unit at Roehampton to be properly kitted out with his new limbs. I missed him terribly and tried to forget him. But he wouldn't let me. Now he was not embarrassed to express his feelings for me. He wrote wonderful, loving letters to me and urged me to visit him on my day off.

I lived for those weekends and Raymond and I grew closer. He was soft, kind and gentle, and always brave. He fought so hard to come to terms with his disabilities. And I helped him, not just to accept them, but to fight them as well, to overcome them so that he could live as normal a life as possible. We were totally bound up with each other; mentally and physically we were so compatible. Although we did not make love, our gentle petting satisfied us both at that stage.

Ray worked hard to master his new legs and he made excellent progress in his quest to walk again. Soon he was attending a rehabilitation centre to train as an accountant and he would arrive to meet me from work in a blue three-wheeled invalid car which he handled very well. In this little vehicle, we took long rides out into the country when the weather was fine. When it wasn't, we just stayed at the hospital and played cards in the nurses' sitting room.

During this period, I often thought about what the future held for us. Every time I saw Ray now, I would feel passionate stirrings in my stomach and I knew that I was deeply in love with him. But what could I expect from our relationship? I had no idea. Ray was severely disabled and might even be sexually impotent. If that were so, then how could we marry? And would he be able to support himself financially? But in spite of all these nagging doubts, I knew in my heart of hearts that one day I would be his.

One bright, sunny afternoon Ray arrived in his little blue car looking even jollier than ever. As he grinned at me my heart jumped. How handsome he was with that impish face and a mop of tousled hair!

'I've got a surprise for you, Jenny,' he said. 'Well, in fact, I've got two . . .' he added mysteriously.

'Oh, tell me, then. Don't keep me in suspense . . .'

But Ray only grinned at me. I got in the car and we drove a good way into the country before he told me, 'Darling, I've got a job, a proper full-time, well-paid job in an accountant's office in town.'

I was thrilled for him. 'Oh, Ray, you'll be independent at last!' But I was immediately concerned for him. 'You won't strain your eyesight, will you, Ray? Make sure you always have good lighting . . .'

Ray squeezed my hand tight. 'Hush, Jenny, don't

spoil things with fussing. Now, soon I'll be able to show you my other surprise.' He turned the car down a little track which ran down to the river.

'Where *are* we going?' I asked.

'Wait and see,' Ray said teasingly.

And that was the day when he first showed me our heavenly riverside abode of love.

Parking the car under an oak tree, we got out and walked down towards the flowing river. The moss on the ground was bright green, as were the leaves on the trees. There was a little clearing to which Ray led me. Waving his arm, he said, 'This is all mine – ours. An uncle of mine died recently and he left me this in his will. He left me this land, that shed, the fishing boat and fishing rights!'

As I stared in wonderment at this place of beauty, Ray turned to me. 'Jenny, we'll share it; we'll save all our money, and then get married next spring,' he said. 'And we'll build our house here.'

His excitement was catching. I laughed with delight at his plans, which included me so totally, and hugged him tight. Ray pulled me closer and kissed me hungrily.

That afternoon we spent exploring our land as if it were a new country. We walked around the property, dipped our hands in the river and inspected the shed. It was just a little shack, really, but it was in that shack, the closest thing to a shared home we had, that Ray and I became lovers.

It wasn't easy. Both Ray and I had inhibitions to overcome. We were both shy; Ray's handicaps made him self-conscious and I felt acutely embarrassed about my plumpness. But as we began to relax and shyly, at first, explore each other's nakedness, we learned and grew together in those precious moments until we consummated our love fully and joyously as we became one.

At every opportunity we would go to our natural home by the river. We dug a patch and began to cultivate our own little garden and when we were there we would cook a meal over a wood fire and eat it while planning our future house, right down to the last nail and picture above the wooden mantelpiece.

Today when I sit by the riverbank I shall recall the heavenly smell of that fire. As unchecked tears fall down my cheeks I shall remember Ray on those glorious weekend trips. And, as always, I shall know that Ray is with me and that everything will be right again. I shall be able to return to my job and home feeling uplifted after a few hours in that one spot where I can find spiritual comfort. For a short while, at least, I will no longer be a lonely, hard-working spinster, but instead a young girl, carefree, happy and hopelessly in love.

Today a soft summer wind cools me as I reach the crest of the hill. I am puffing slightly for I am now in my late thirties and am beginning to feel my age. As I slowly top the hill, I get my first, long-awaited glimpse of the Thames, the long silver strip of river that curves away towards the smoky spires of London. Every time I see this sight I hold my breath. And in the near distance, at the end of the valley lying before me, I can see elm trees. As my bike bumps down the hill and along the leaf-strewn path, I begin to enjoy again the hidden, secret feeling of my love for Ray.

But wait, today something is different. As I approach the land, I can smell burning wood. I am confused. The smell reminds me of those makeshift Sunday meals long ago and my heart leaps. But no, now I can hear the laughter of children, something that was not part of my former life; and there is the unmistakable chatter of women.

I stop my bike and hesitate. I am afraid to venture further. But I have to. Gathering my courage I go forward slowly. Then, to my amazement, I see that in the middle of my wild grass is pitched a bright orange tent. Its vivid colour screams at me. Under one of the trees I see a field kitchen, with a Primus stove, pots and pans, and a washing line strung up with swimming costumes and towels.

Two women are sitting by the river talking, and in the water a man and two boys are playing with a ball. From the sound of their loud laughter, which drifts on the breeze, it is obvious that they are all enjoying themselves.

The scene shocks me. Quite apart from being unexpected, it seems thoroughly modern, loud and vulgar. None of it is a part of my life anywhere, and least of all here in this precious place bordered by the trees and the river, my coveted place of memories with Ray.

I hardly know what to do. I get off my bike and sink down in my usual spot on a mound of long grass. There I sit, chin in hand, gazing down river. And nobody even looks in my direction. I try to conjure up past scenes here on the bank but my feelings of nostalgia, the gentle bitter-sweet self-pity I revel in, will not come today. The feelings are dead. I am furious. How dare these people invade my life and land!

The two boys run by in dripping-wet briefs. They give me a quick glance and giggle.

I blush. What are they laughing at? How dare they! But I am timid and cannot pluck up the courage to tell them that they are all trespassing.

Suddenly my attention is caught by the swan and her cygnets. I have been watching these babes carefully ever since their first appearance in the early spring. On every visit I have watched the majestic mother as she floats towards the shore, her flotilla of young floating with military precision behind. The mother gives a protective hiss as she comes near, but graciously allows the young ones to pick up the crumbs I throw into the dark olive water.

I hear a rustle behind me. Turning around, I see the two small boys, having spotted the swan, come tearing down the bank with excited yells. The swan hisses fiercely and stretches out her neck in anger.

'Mind, it might go for yer,' the older boy yells in a delightful cockney tone.

'Won't 'urt yer, sissy!' says the other lad defiantly.

I decide to intervene. The children are obviously Londoners and don't know how dangerous a swan can be. 'Don't go any closer,' I call. 'A mother swan can be extremely dangerous,' I warn. I hold out my bag of bread. 'Here, feed them some crumbs. Throw the bread just in front of them.'

But the swan has decided it is time to go. Gathering up her brood, she drifts serenely away.

The boys have gone back to their play, and I find my memories creeping back. Soon I am lost in daydream, stroking the bark of the tree where Raymond's boat used to be tied. Tears fill my eyes. I want desperately to throw my arms around that willow tree and weep with it, just as I have often done in the past. But with these strangers nearby, I must restrain my grief.

I wipe the tears away quickly, as a river bus approaches, carrying its hoard of holidaymakers off to Oxford. People wave at me but I do not feel like waving back.

Now the little boys have returned. The elder one chirps, 'My mum says would you like a cup of tea?'

'That's very kind of you,' I reply with a smile. They are nice boys. They dash away but in no time they have returned, creeping almost snail-like as they balance the steaming cup of tea and a plate of biscuits. I sip the delicious hot, sweet liquid as the boys park themselves one either side of me. We start to chat.

Although I thought one was older than the other, it turns out that the boys are twins. They are called Tom and Rob, and they are nine.

'We're on our 'olidays,' Tom informs me.

'And our boat broke down,' chants Rob. 'Ain't it smashing 'ere?'

'We live in London. There ain't nuffin there like 'ere. I wish I lived here . . .'

'You can't . . .' says his brother. 'Don't belong to us.'

'Well, who does it belong to then?' Tom challenges his twin.

Rob shrugs. 'Dunno, some fat old millionaire, s'pose.'

I listen to their banter but I don't enlighten them. Their remarks have set me thinking: I wonder how many other children like them would love to play in just such a place as this.

For the next few hours I just sit on the bank and watch the children enjoying themselves so freely. How delightful that they can appreciate the beauty around them and derive so much pleasure from it. My mind is busily milling over thoughts that are cropping up in my head.

By the time I leave, a distinct idea is forming in my mind. The cockney families wave me goodbye. As I go, I realize that I have enjoyed the river today much more than I have for a long time. Can this possibly be because for once I haven't allowed myself to wallow in misery?

As I cycle home through the twilight I think of little Tom and Rob, snug in their sleeping bags in that bright tent. Yes, the land provides an ideal spot for camping. Am I terribly selfish, I wonder, to hang on to this isolated open space for myself when the cities are so overcrowded? Others could appreciate it, too . . .

I find myself going over and over basic assumptions I have clung on to for too long. That dream house of mine and Ray's will never be built, I have to accept that. I could never afford it on my salary. And besides, will I really want to live in such a lonely spot all on my own? Such plans were made when Ray and I had a future together.

A development company not so long ago offered a huge price to buy the land from me. But I refused. It was impossible for me to part with it. But that night I argued with myself about it. 'You're almost middle-aged, Jenny,' I reasoned. 'You have no kin, and it's time to put your house in order.' But selling our land would be going too far, I knew that. No, I could never part with the precious place where Ray and I had shared so much and loved one another so completely.

My thoughts drift back to that first August when the red runner-bean flowers had fallen to expose tiny beans. I was so thrilled at the beginning of our own vegetable garden. 'Ray, look!' I cried. 'Real beans! Our very own! Our own creation!' Ray came towards me. He was sun-tanned and very fit looking.

'And look what I've grown,' he said triumphantly, holding up an earth-covered bunch of radishes for me to admire.

I hugged him. 'Oh, Ray,' I murmured. 'I feel that I've got everything in the world I could possibly wish for.'

In my happiness I had forgotten the old Irish saying that one should not court the devil. I wonder now if that is what I did.

But everything did seem perfect that day: our vegetables thriving, Ray with a steady job, our savings mounting up, and the go-ahead from the council to build our own home. We had even decided earlier that day to get married one weekend in the autumn.

Matron was rather put out when I resigned the next day. 'I had hoped you would be sensible enough to stay until the new year, Jenny,' she said rather sternly. 'The winter is always a desperately hard time to keep staff, with flu epidemics and all.'

I thought about Matron's comments and decided that she was right. Perhaps I was being a bit hasty and perhaps we could put off our wedding until the spring. Later, when I talked to Ray about this he agreed with me to delay our plans. But he also seemed sad that afternoon, and I noticed he was not moving about with his usual assurance, either.

'Ray, tell me what's wrong?' I asked anxiously.

We had always been very honest with each other, and now he turned to me and told me resignedly, 'I have been having a lot of migraines recently. There are many days when I can't even go to work the pain is so bad.' To my horror, he suddenly broke down. 'Oh Jenny,' he cried, clutching me tight, 'I'm so scared.'

I stroked his hair and reassured him but I knew that something serious was wrong with him.

I persuaded him to go back to the hospital for a check-up, and the following weekend Ray gave me the bad news. There was to be no more work for him. He had been told to wear dark glasses and get plenty of rest and that he needed a minor operation which had been scheduled for December. If all went well, then his sight would be saved. We both tried hard not to be despondent and certainly never discussed what would happen if all did not go well.

Not long after this discovery, Ray announced that

he wanted to move to his patch of land and live in the little shack and have me visit at weekends. 'It's ever so peaceful here and I'll save money not having to pay rent,' he reasoned, and I agreed with him. I still believed that everything would be all right and that our dream house would still be built in the years to come. It would have lots of bedrooms, a nursery full of children and a pretty patio from which to admire our blooming garden. I fall asleep with this memory swimming around my head.

The next morning I make myself a cup of tea and look at my desk. There is a pile of unopened correspondence, most of it I know comes from parents, some complaining, others with almost impossible requests. But among these letters is a posh buff envelope. I know what it is. It is another missive from the solicitor acting for the development company which is so anxious to buy my little patch of land. I open it and gasp. The price they first offered me has been trebled. Why, with all *that* money I could give up work and travel abroad. But a little tug of despair stops my fantasies. After all, whom would I travel with? And without the children here at the home to look after, I would be even more alone than ever.

As I sit at my desk with my tea going cold in the cup, I think hard. I know that now is the time to make a decision. 'You can't hold on to memories forever,' I say to myself. And I know Ray would agree with that. He always looked ahead to the future. I can hear him now, as if calling me from somewhere beyond space and time.

I close my eyes and bathe my tired mind in memories of him. That summer passed without mishap, but then Ray became adamant about staying in the shack all winter. I thought this a very bad idea but Ray ignored all my pleadings for him to change his mind. He did not care if the winter was cold, wet and very lonely. I resigned myself to his stubborn position and helped him prepare for the icy winter.

Together we collected firewood, sawing up logs and stacking them in great piles. I brought lots of warm blankets for the bed and powdered cocoa for Ray to drink before going to sleep – a substitute for me, I laughed.

One afternoon, after hours of hard work, we sat down to gallons of tea and toasted muffins which tasted of wood smoke. Ray sat back in his chair with a contented sigh. 'I've been thinking,' he said. 'Perhaps we should get married in secret. As long as you keep it a secret from your boss, there won't be a problem. You could continue your work until we build our house in the spring.'

Any hesitation I might have had was swept away when he added, 'I want to feel that you really belong to me and I don't want to wait any longer to do that.'

So we did it. We got married in the town register office in the middle of November. We grabbed two passers-by from the street who acted as our witnesses. We wanted no one to spoil our secret. I had bought a blue nylon suit from a chain store and borrowed a hat from the girl I shared a room with.

It was a quick and quiet event. There was no

champagne, no photographs and no congratulatory telegrams. All we had was a pot of tea and a chocolate swiss roll, which we shared as we sat huddled up to the log fire in our home – the shack. Oh, we were so happy! Honeymooners on a Caribbean cruise could not have been happier.

The next Monday I returned to the hospital. I was sad at our parting but felt warmed by an inner glow. I was now Mrs Beharrel, and that meant a lot to me. I was content to rush home to my husband, yes, my *husband*, every weekend, taking with me small provisions for our little home.

The only cloud in our blue sky was Ray's eyesight. I noticed in small ways that it seemed to be getting worse – a sudden clumsiness here or a faltering step there. We never spoke about it, though. I prayed that his scheduled eye operation would make everything all right. It was as if we knew we had so little time left together and did not want to spoil any of it. We just wanted to enjoy every moment to the full. But each time I left Ray to get back to town, the same feeling of dread filled my heart. But I knew I could not stay with him all the time. We had agreed that I should work until the spring, and our shortage of money and need to save up settled it. There was no other way, but even so I have always felt a shameful guilt about Ray's death.

Until December the weather had been mild. Suddenly it changed, bringing strong ugly winds and freezing temperatures. Then it teemed with icy rain for days on end. At the hospital things were hectic and

I was unable to get away one weekend as so many patients were admitted suffering from influenza or hypothermia. I was very upset but we were so short-staffed that I had to stay and work. It was two weeks before I could get away on my bicycle to visit my husband in our shack.

The icy rain never let up and the wind took my breath away as I left the sheltered confines of the hospital. But I had to go to Raymond. There was an empty space inside me which only he could fill. The following week, Ray was due to go to London for a preliminary eye operation, so it might be weeks before we could meet again in our little shack. As I forced the bicycle pedals round, fighting the wind and rain, I kept a picture in my mind of Ray with his bright fire, hot tea and loving arms.

I knew something was wrong the minute I turned down the lane. A strange sense of desolation filled me as I rode in. The river was swirling angrily, green and frothy. The tide was high and the swollen waters swept over the landing stage, lashing the spare boat monotonously against the bank. Even the weeping willow's roots, which were usually well exposed, were drowned in the thrashing waters. And the branches themselves were bent down lower than I had ever seen them.

Dismounting, I gave a low shudder and ran towards the shack, dropping my bicycle in the mud. But there was no welcoming glow of lamplight, and no trail of smoke wound its way up the battered chimney. Everything was cold and silent.

Where was Ray? I was shivering as much from fear

as from cold. I knew something was terribly wrong. 'Ray, where are you, darling?' I called. But the wind blew my words back into my face. My frozen fingers were stiff from holding the handlebars. I lit up the oil lamp by the front door. The door had been left open so Ray could not be far away. The bed was unmade and on the table lay a bowl, which had clearly contained Ray's breakfast of cornflakes, a teapot full of cold tea and Ray's large mug which we had gaily bought together in a junk shop. The mug had a funny face on one side, but as I looked at it now it seemed to be grinning evilly at me.

The sight of that face on the mug made me panic and I ran out into the storm. The trees groaned in the roaring wind and their branches thrashed in the air. Mud clung to my boots. I slipped and slithered on the grass as I searched frantically around the garden for Ray. Then I tried to get back under control. Perhaps Ray had gone into town and been held up by the storm. Yes, that was the obvious explanation for his absence. But when I opened the garage doors there was Ray's blue car. It was the only means of transport Ray had. All feelings of reassurance had gone. Ray *had* to be near the shack somewhere.

I dashed down to the river, tripping and sliding as I went. Wading in the foot-high waters which had burst the bank, I made my way to the willow where Ray's favourite boat was usually moored. The boat had gone and the broken rope blew about in the wind, catching every now and then in the branches of the tree. There was a large hole in the bank and all the boards that held a temporary landing stage Ray had been building had disappeared. I was gripped by sheer terror. Throwing myself flat, I plunged my arms elbowdeep into the freezing water. 'Ray! Ray!' I yelled. 'Where are you? Ray, my love . . .'

The howling of the wind was my only answer.

I don't like remembering the rest of the night. It comes back now as a hazy blur of blackness, a nightmare, and sheer terror.

I left my job at the hospital for a stay in a nursing home after suffering a nervous breakdown. At the inquest the verdict was accidental death by drowning, but the publicity was awful. Several papers implied that I had murdered Ray. The fact that I had inherited the land and shack after such a short marriage was just too good to be true for those scandal-mongers who did not care if they ruined a life more than it was ruined already. And some even implied that only someone with an ulterior motive would marry a man so disabled as Ray.

For a year I hid away, scared even to visit the shack. Then, one bright and warm spring day reminded me of the first time Ray had taken me to the land. I found the courage to return and sat by the riverbank. There I lapped up the sweet silence and the sense of peace. And there I found my Ray again and he helped nurse me back to health. Whenever I felt low, I would visit Ray again and again to revive my spirits.

I took up a specialized children's nursing course and obtained the position in the disabled children's home where I now work. For many years I have kept my lonely but peaceful vigil beside the very river which swept away my love.

But tonight I feel different. I feel strong and healed, ready to move on to the next stage of my life. I know that I can make up my mind at last about what to do with the land. Should I sell to the development company or let the place rot? I am happy again at last. I know what I shall do and it will be neither of these things. Best of all, I know Ray will approve of my final choice, which will make many other people happy too.

Moonections

A heavy silver moon hung over the heaving spring tide which tossed and surged wildly in the strong winds that night.

Dr Stella Howard stood at the window of her cottage listening to the crash and roar of the waves as they dashed over the high sea wall. And in the background she could hear the monotonous call from the lighthouse warning the brave or the foolhardy that there were rocks ahead for those who risked the dangers of the sea on such a stormy night.

Stella had always been thrilled by the sea storms around this lonely shore and tonight was no exception. In fact the delicious flutter of fear in her breast was the first time she had been jolted from the dullness of her depression for a long time. Perhaps her cottage would be swept away this time, with her in it, and solve the problems that weighed so heavily down on her now. And, although always proud of her rational nature, she allowed herself to believe that something mysterious and irrational was about to happen.

It had been Stella's own choice to hide out in this sequestered house, a disused coastguard's cottage. It was here she intended to stay until the disease took its toll, away from anxious relatives, inquisitive friends, and concerned colleagues. Here there was no need to smile and look brave, or to weep and demand sympathy. Out here on the lonely marsh it was easy to live each day for its own simple value. With the spring flowers in the garden – the winter aconites, crocuses and snowdrops – and the wild birds on the shore, Stella could let life flow past and not worry.

There were plenty of times when she lost faith, when her internal armour dissolved and anxious worries overpowered her. At times like that she would wonder if she should stop fighting the fears and let them rule her life, which would end within a year anyway. Should she resist this unstoppable force or simply accept that it was going to get her in the end anyway? And what about the decision to come out to live in this remote cottage? Was that a sensible thing to do? Was it wise to try to disappear from it all?

But even these questions were pointless. It served no purpose now to dwell on such things.

'I must stop this nonsense,' she told herself, pulling out a large white handkerchief and giving her nose a terrific blow. 'Remember that you are a scientist, you are a logical person at all times.'

Suddenly, outside the house, she heard a strange and terrifying sound. It was a peculiar sloshing and swishing that she had never heard before. The noise came in rapidly from the direction of the sea, roared over the roof, and then seemed to slow down among the old apple trees in the orchard at the back. Even now she could hear a continuous hissing and belching of a most unearthly order.

Stella felt the blood run from her face and her knees went weak. She was very frightened but she kept telling herself that there had to be some simple explanation for this unidentifiable noise. She forced herself to open the back door to see what was going on. Leaving the door open, and pulling her cardigan around her against the strong wind, she ran down the garden to the orchard.

The wild wind whipped her dress tightly about her legs and her hair came loose and streamed out behind her as she stood staring up into the old apple trees. There, up in the branches of the biggest and oldest tree, rested a strange round object. It seemed to pulsate, moving up and down rhythmically, puffing air or gas of some sort out of a large hole in its side. The object gleamed a greeny silver in the moonlight.

Stella relaxed and smiled. 'A weather balloon! So that was what the noise was!' Satisfied by the evidence, she was about to return to the warmth of her cottage when something dropped out of the tree and landed on the ground with a plop. There, at her feet, lay another curious object. It was about three feet long and seemed to be covered with a shining suit of silver-green.

It looks just like a splendid codfish, thought Stella, as she knelt to examine it. It was actually closer to a mermaid with a fish's head. There was an arm, which she picked up. She tried to feel a pulse in the tiny wrist, but she could find no flutter of life. She pulled the oddity into a sitting position, noting how very lightweight it was. It was just like a balloon, too. Too intrigued by the object to be afraid, she picked it up and ran with it back to her cottage, not bothering to take another look up at the other strange objects in the apple trees.

Placing the shape on the couch, she got out her sharp surgical scissors and nipped the skin-like hood that covered the head. Her senses were now very alert. She concentrated hard as she set about doing this, totally absorbed by the examination. The skin-like helmet fell away, revealing a perfect human head. There was a small-featured pink face surrounded by a halo of golden curls. The tightly closed eyes were fringed with long golden lashes.

Stella stepped back in amazement, staring down at this small thing of beauty. It was lifeless. Her training prompted her to bend down and put her lips directly onto the little bow-shaped mouth and breathe the kiss of life into that fish-like body. Her head swam as she did so. A thrilling giddy sensation rushed through her, an emotion she had almost forgotten.

Then the smooth white eyelids flickered and two brilliant blue eyes stared up at her in confusion. The little mouth twitched and noises came from the throat. They were low, unintelligible sounds, but something about them was definitely human. The little hand moved slowly towards a slit in the skin suit. Stella moved back warily, wondering if it was reaching for some kind of defensive weapon. But instead of a weapon, the hand reached inside the skin and pulled out a long tube full of capsules. The creature then proceeded to empty the tube into its mouth. Almost immediately, the creature began to grow and grow, filling out like a steadily inflated balloon. It, or he, began to look quite solid. It moved its limbs about and struggled slightly to sit up.

Stella took off her spectacles and wiped raindrops from the lenses. As she stared with undisguised inquisitiveness at this little figure, the little man – for it now looked very like a little man – looked back at her with equal curiosity.

'Well, I never,' Stella cried. 'What are you, fish or human?' She was still too astonished to be afraid of the situation.

The little visitor frowned at the traces of a smile on Stella's face. He clearly did not find his predicament quite so amusing. He pulled himself to his feet and drew himself up to full height (just reaching Stella's waist), and opened his little mouth to speak. 'I am an explorer from the planet Moonecticus,' he said in a surprisingly deep sing-song voice. His accent, Stella noticed, was perfect. 'This, I understand, is the planet Earth, so you must be one of Earth's inhabitants, a human.' He stared at her with those perfect blue eyes.

'An explorer?' repeated Stella in a soft voice, 'From Moonecticus . . .'

The creature looked at her somewhat impatiently as if she were being slow and stupid. 'Where are my brothers?' he suddenly demanded in a strident voice.

'You mean, there are more of you?' cried Stella. She was indeed feeling rather slow and stupid. She went to the back door and opened it. The light from the house illuminated the grass lawn where two other little fish-shapes lay. The little man pushed past her and marched up to his companions. He barked out a strange order and the others immediately released the skin-like hoods to reveal similar cherubic faces. Then, as their companion had done, from long tubes they both swallowed pills. They expanded and inflated like balloons, and within moments they too had become solid.

Speechless with wonder, Stella watched these creatures as they now all three stood in line and bowed low. They were identical to look at.

'These are my brothers,' said the first fellow. 'But I am the leader,' he added quickly, just to clarify the situation for her.

Stella nodded affirmatively. 'Good God!' she muttered under her breath. 'I hope I'm not dreaming . . .'

All three creatures smiled sweetly at her. She smiled back. 'Welcome to my house, gentlemen,' she said. 'My name is Stella, Dr Stella Howard.'

All three nodded at her and then marched solemnly past her and inside the house. Stella closed the door. The little men looked around the room inquisitively and backed away from the blazing fire in the hearth.

'We don't like too much heat,' explained the leader. 'Have we your permission to remove our travel suits?'

Stella sat down at the dining table, her chin in her hands. She was fascinated. 'Do just as you wish,' she said. 'Don't mind me.'

Slowly and carefully the men stripped off the skin suits and packed them up carefully as one might a parachute. Then, from concealed pockets, they produced several tubes of pills and a minute radio. The three little men sat cross-legged in a circle on the floor. Stella listened, fascinated, as the small moon men told of their journey through space.

'Our journey to the planet Earth is not an accident,' said the leader. 'We have planned to come here for many years. We have been able to pick up signals from Earth for a long time, so we have always known of your existence. And, of course, many, many decades ago, Earth men came to our planet.'

Stella was astonished. 'I never heard of that,' she said. 'That fact has never been made public.'

'I can assure you that it is true,' the little man said. 'Perhaps you don't know about it because in a sense it was a failed mission. Those Earth men never returned home. We three are their descendants and that is why we have been chosen for this trip.'

'This is all extraordinary,' cried Stella. 'I have to believe what you're saying. Otherwise I must be crazy.'

'We are all brothers from the same seed,' continued the leader. 'We all feel the same pain, the same joy. The only difference between them and me is that I am fully male and they are bisexual. Fortunately, they love each other so they do not breed,' he added.

Stella was puzzled by his last remark. 'So males and females breed in the normal way on your planet?' she asked.

The creature nodded. 'Yes, and we have more than two species. In fact, this is why we are on this mission. We have come with a definite purpose – to find an answer to our over-population problem,' he explained.

'You mean there are too many of you,' Stella said, somewhat pointlessly.

He nodded. 'There are many many millions of us, far too many. Our planet is so overcrowded that our resources are running out fast. Now it is imperative that we do something very soon to avoid famine.'

'But do you not have any means of birth control? And what is the natural life expectancy of your people?' Stella fired questions as she found her curiosity rising.

'Oh, some die,' the visitor explained, 'but only at a great age, because sickness is something that we have conquered. In his lifetime one male will produce on average a hundred children and our females produce in multiple births. They have at least ten offspring at a time.'

'Good heavens!' cried Stella. 'No wonder you're worried about over-population.' She plied them with questions, so anxious was she now to learn about the planet of Moonecticus.

The travellers happily continued to inform her. 'Our planet is smaller than Earth, and two light-years' distance away. Our way of life is not unlike your own, as far as I can tell,' said one of the brothers. 'But having made your acquaintance our research will be easier now, I feel.'

Stella sat and listened, chin in hand, spellbound by their little sing-song voices.

'As you may have observed,' said the leader, 'we are not naturally of a solid substance as you Earth dwellers are, but that is because of the lightness of the air on our planet. It was my brother,' he said, pointing to one of the other two, 'who discovered a means of acquiring this heaviness which is necessary for us to survive here. My other brother invented the ship that carried us through space.' Stella smiled at the bisexual brothers who nodded excitedly and emitted in unison a strange sound which could have been either giggling or sobbing.

'We can survive here only for a short time,' said the leader. 'We must repair our ship as the solar battery on board will be needed for us to return through space.'

'So you intend to go home again soon?' asked Stella.

He nodded. 'As soon as our mission is accomplished. It may be the last chance for our planet. We *have* to find an answer to our population problem or we will all starve and die out.'

'Here on Earth, we have a war every generation. That's one way of keeping the population down,' said Stella drily.

'War?' The traveller looked puzzled. 'Please explain.'

Stella was amazed by his innocence. 'Do you mean to tell me that even with those surplus millions you have never tried to destroy each other, that you haven't killed each other in an effort to grab resources?'

The traveller stared at her. 'If you are asking if we take each other's lives, the answer is no,' he said emphatically.

'You don't kill? You have no weapons?' she asked, incredulously.

He shook his head. 'When we left, the dark years were just beginning. This is when the planet passes out of the sun's orbit. During this period many will go to the burning mountain and dispose of themselves – whole families, in fact. But it is always of their own free-will. The most altruistic do this as their contribution to the planet's good.'

'Mass suicide,' murmured Stella. 'How interesting.' Reaching into a drawer, she pulled out a small notebook and began to scribble down the extraordinary description of this other planet and its customs.

When she had finished, she put down her pencil and looked at her visitors. 'One thing puzzles me,' she said. 'Why don't these dark years with their mass suicides keep the population of your planet down?'

The travellers looked resignedly at each other. 'Because those that stay breed more during the dark years,' the leader said with a sigh.

'So the suicides are pointless then,' Stella added. The three little men nodded in unison.

Stella glanced at her watch. It was very late. 'Look here, it will be daylight soon,' she said. 'I for one need some sleep. We had better get our heads down. There's a bed under the stairs over there. You are welcome to that.'

When Stella awoke the next morning, she was pleased to see that the storm had abated. Now she could just hear the gentle slap of the waves on the shore. The warm sun was reflecting a leafy pattern on the wall as it peeped through the creeper-covered windows.

She yawned sleepily and sat up. Suddenly she remembered the bizarre conversation she had been having with the space travellers, and felt a surge of disappointment at the realization that it had just been a dream.

The house was as silent as a graveyard. Apart from the waves the only other sound was of the cows lowing on the marsh. Admonishing herself for being so silly and sentimental, Stella slipped on her robe and went to the window. But there, in the garden, were the three little space travellers huddled together in the apple tree inspecting their curious spacecraft. Stella smiled broadly at the welcome sight. It had not been a dream after all!

In the clear morning air the sun's rays shone down on three golden heads. It was all too unbelievable. Stella pinched herself several times before she was convinced that she had not, after all, been dreaming and that the encounter she had thought she had had, did actually happen.

Well, the newspapers would love this, wouldn't they? *Real* space travellers here on Earth, creatures they would not have to invent. But then she suddenly thought how little she wanted anyone else to know about her new friends – the publicity would ruin what was left of her life. Her privacy would be invaded, journalists would be crawling around the gardens, crowds would gather . . . Never again could she face that hullabaloo!

Stella had devoted most of her working life to liberating women from the burden of unwanted children. She had battled for many years against religious bigots and reactionary groups, always believing that her contribution could do nothing but help humanity. It was fate that had brought these space travellers here to see Stella, she who had been a leading member of the research team that had launched the birth control pill. That pill revolutionized women's lives, giving them the choice about how many children to have, and thus giving them a real choice between a meaningful life of their own and a premature death. Until the widespread availability of the pill, women's lives were not their own. It was an achievement that Stella was greatly proud of, and with good reason.

Was it fate, their appearance? Did those little creatures know that much of the knowledge they sought was lying there in this Earth woman's brain? Did they know that they need go no further to seek the information essential for reforming their planet? Well, she would help them as much as she could. She had little more to offer her own society, but perhaps she could make a contribution towards the improvement of theirs.

The three little men were walking towards her as Stella opened the back door. They came three abreast, without the skin suits. Now they were wearing short white shifts, and the wind blew their golden curls. 'Like little angels,' muttered Stella, as she watched them.

They greeted her with big smiles.

'I'm going to make some coffee,' she told them. Placing some coffee beans in the grinder, she turned the handle. 'You should try some.'

The visitors examined the coffee beans and they stared intently, fascinated as the brown liquid bubbled and frothed in the percolator.

'Is this your sacred beverage?' asked the leader.

'Well,' Stella grinned, 'I suppose you could call it that.'

'We would be most honoured to partake of your national drink,' he informed her.

'Are you sure your bodies will be able to process this substance?' Stella asked, suddenly concerned for their health and welfare.

'It will be quite safe to try it,' replied the traveller. 'On Moonecticus we eat and drink, as do all humans. But we came here with sufficient energy stored inside us and with plenty of vitamins, just in case there was nothing here for us to eat, or only strange food which might disagree with our digestive systems which are extremely delicate. We do not consume animal flesh and only drink sweet water, but your famous coffee we would like to try.'

It was a long time since Stella had laughed so heartily. Their enthusiasm and interest really amused her. No golden communion-cup at the highest church festival was ever passed by so gentle hands as Stella's huge mug of coffee was passed round that kitchen. Each little traveller took a sip with a very ceremonious gesture, each little head nodded its approval and returned the mug to her which she accepted with equal grace.

With the ceremony over, the leader turned solemnly to Stella. 'Where are all the other inhabitants of this world? So far I've seen none but yourself.'

Stella smiled. 'This is only a minute fragment of this huge world. It's solitary and away from the crowds. That's exactly why I live here.'

'Then we must travel on,' he said. 'We must if our mission is to be accomplished.'

Stella looked worried. 'It's very tough out there and you are essentially three frail little men who know less than nothing about our planet,' she said. 'How will you survive?'

'We are very strong and will survive for a while whatever happens to us,' replied the leader.

'Earth men are beasts, they will tear you apart,' Stella warned with some passion.

But they were not to be deterred. 'We must repair our ship and travel on,' he said firmly.

Stella could see that he was not to be swayed. She stared sympathetically at this small, frail creature who was such a dedicated pioneer. 'Oh, well, all right,' she shrugged, 'but we must retrieve your ship from the tree. Then you can repair it in the barn. I'll have to move my car out, but you are welcome to it.'

'That is most kind of you, we are extremely grateful.' Their good manners were delightful to Stella.

'I have begun to feel responsible for you little cherubs,' she laughed. 'What else can I do?'

The four of them worked the whole morning to release that precious spacecraft from the old apple tree and park it safely in the barn. Watching the travellers, Stella realized that, contrary to their appearance, they were, in fact, very strong. They also worked in unison, as if with one mind.

At midday they had slowed down slightly and one of them suddenly lay down on the grass and seemed to shrivel slightly in the hot sunlight. His two brothers carried him into the shade and quickly gave him some pills. These seemed to restore him immediately.

Stella watched in fascination. What wondrous scientific knowledge did these creatures possess?

'We cannot work in the hot sun,' explained the leader. 'We have enough solar energy stored within us. Extra sunlight is only destructive.'

Stella's quick mind was reminded of the way radium

patients are affected by the sun. Was there a similarity here?

In the cool of the evening, Stella walked with the leader to the shore, while the other two brothers excitedly examined Stella's little car.

The leader kept picking up various objects off the beach as a child might – a shell, a dead starfish, some seaweed – and stored them in a tube he carried which was similar to the one that held those life-preserving pills.

'Why do you live alone?' he asked Stella suddenly. 'Have you no male companion?'

Rather taken aback by the forthrightness of the question, Stella answered abruptly: 'No, certainly not!' She realized that she sounded very defensive.

'For a female as young and beautiful as yourself, is it not very surprising?'

Stella smiled and scrutinized him carefully. He was not as naïve as she had thought. 'I'm not as young as you think,' she said quietly, 'and I've not very long to live.' But she felt chuffed by the flattery.

'You mean you will leave this planet Earth?' he asked.

'I'm not sure where I will go, but I do know that I have an incurable progressive disease that will eventually destroy me,' she replied.

The leader stood still, looking up at her in concern. 'Do you suffer pain?'

'Sometimes,' she nodded.

'Then I can help,' he said in a matter-of-fact tone. 'For we have mastered pain on Moonecticus.'

Stella smiled. 'I'm trying to believe you,' she said. 'But it's hard.'

The traveller held out two tiny hands. 'Take hold of them,' he said. 'Blank all thoughts from your mind. There is no reason why our healing power should not protect you, too.'

Puzzled but excited, Stella reached out and took those tiny warm hands in her own. The creature's blue eyes turned towards the sun. As he stood there, strange thrills ran up her arm, into her chest and then her heart. A tiny electric current seemed to black out her mind for a few seconds.

'That's it,' the leader told her as he released her. 'Now you will gradually recover.'

Stella certainly felt different. She felt light and buoyant, and strong feelings of well-being washed over her. The medical profession did not entirely dismiss spiritual healing, although it was generally sceptical about it. But have they mastered this secret on Moonecticus? she wondered.

They moved on and began to trot briskly along the sands. Then they broke into a run. 'I can't believe it,' Stella cried, 'only yesterday walking was an effort.'

'We are in some ways more advanced than you Earthlings,' the leader said thoughtfully. He paused and then added, 'When I travel on, I shall always remember you.' He spoke quietly and from the heart.

Stella felt touched and was suddenly over-whelmed with sadness. She did not want him to go away. Impatiently she pushed the feeling from her. How ridiculous to have such feelings about an alien creature!

They sat down by the breakwater. Stella felt very confused. She did not draw away when the traveller's soft tiny hand stroked the back of her neck.

'Be happy,' he said. 'Don't look so sad.'

Stella looked quickly at that pretty boy-like face beside her. How foolish she was, they were like children. It was her duty to protect them from this wicked world.

'It might not be possible to re-fly your machine over this planet,' she said, trying to ignore the warm feeling generated by his stroking hand.

'That is our problem,' he shrugged. 'We took that risk when we came.'

'There are a lot of places where they will shoot you out of the air,' she warned. 'Why not leave the ship here and I will come with you and help you to explore this land at least.' Something she had read in the paper that morning had given her an idea.

'We cannot travel far from our ship,' he said. 'When the pills are gone we must depend on our store of solar energy for survival.'

'It's only about two hours' drive to the capital,' Stella explained. 'And it's easy to return if things go wrong.'

The traveller considered Stella's idea and then nodded. 'All right,' he said. 'It's up to you. We trust you implicitly.'

'I want to take you somewhere that might be of interest to you,' she said enigmatically.

'And it would be nice to enjoy your hospitality a while longer,' he added sweetly.

'Come, my friend,' she smiled. 'Let's get organized.'

The light in Stella's coastguard cottage was on all night. The shepherd out on the marsh observed it but he went about his business unconcerned. Had he peered in through a window, he could have seen a strange scene in the warm red glow of the lamp. He would have seen Dr Stella Howard, glasses on the end of her nose, hair awry, working at an ancient sewing machine. Around her, her three small, strange guests chattered like happy children at a party. With less than dextrous hands, Stella pushed material under the needle while the little golden-haired creature stood beside her and turned the handle.

Stella was making clothes for her companions so that they would not be too conspicuous when she took them around London. With some ingenuity, she altered some of her own garments to fit their tiny frames.

They were all dressed like children or youths. One wore a roll-necked jersey and a shortened skirt in the uniform of a modern schoolgirl. Another was dressed in a velvet trouser suit, cut down, and a frilly blouse. He had the distinctive appearance of a youth from the King's Road. The third one, in Stella's best navy suit, looked very smart. Stella had sighed as she reluctantly cut the legs short and tapered them to fit his little legs. 'I must be mad,' she grumbled, taking off her glasses and rubbing her tired eyes. 'I won't have a decent suit left.'

'We are most grateful,' said the leader, as he rubbed his face gently on hers as a pet kitten might. Stella smiled. At least her efforts were very much appreciated.

'Oh, you are all so sweet and it's been such fun,' she laughed. 'I hope tomorrow will go as well.'

'Tomorrow, when the sun rises, I will renew your energy, my lovely Earth woman,' said the leader, his arms about her neck.

Stella felt exhilarated. What did these little child-men do to her? In some way, they awakened a maternal instinct that had been lying dormant in her barren body for all these years. 'I must get some sleep,' she murmured. 'Or I'll be fit for nothing tomorrow.'

'Sleep peacefully,' murmured the leader. 'We'll rouse you at dawn with some coffee.'

In the morning, the travellers swam naked in the sea, coming ashore in their fresh clean skins. They seemed to dry very quickly, and their blond hair did the same. After their bathe, they climbed into their new outfits with much excitement. They then lined up before Stella, just waiting to be inspected.

It was going to turn out to be a very exciting day, Stella thought as she drove her red mini towards London, with the three little men all wedged in the back. Along the broad highway they sped, her passengers taking an avid interest in the surroundings, waving friendly greetings at the oncoming traffic.

As they came into London, the space travellers gazed up in wonder at the tall buildings. 'Our dwellings are underground,' explained the leader. 'We have nothing like this on our planet.'

Stella glanced at them in her rearview mirror and was shocked to see one of them lifting his short skirt and exposing his frilly knickers underneath. 'Tell your brother to pull his skirt down.' Oh, dear, she thought, how can they be expected to have any idea about modesty and decency. Perhaps she had better buy this fellow a pair of long trousers before he exposed his knickers to anyone who would be offended. She had always thought the fashion for short skirts quite ridiculous.

Pulling in to a large shopping centre, she parked the car and hustled her charges into a large department store. 'Come on,' she ordered, 'all stay together.'

Obediently they followed her on to the escalator where they huddled together in absolute terror. The other shoppers noticed this odd group with amusement.

Feeling increasingly embarrassed, Stella strode on to the Boys' Department. Although she had asked them to stay close, it proved impossible to get her friends to stay still. They ran around constantly in a state of excitement as they examined this and that, even climbing up on to the display platforms to examine the wax figures with obvious delight.

'Will you kindly keep your children under control!' cried a shop manager.

Stella turned to apologize when she saw the miniskirted traveller wrestling with a shop assistant before disappearing into the lift with a tartan tam-o'-shanter on top of his head.

'Oh my gosh, get him! He'll get lost!' she cried.

They hurried for another lift but there was no sign of him anywhere. One hour later, Stella stood outside the big store. She felt hot, tired and very harassed. The shop had brought out the worst in these little men and she regretted ever taking them there. One of them was still missing and the other two had been stopped by the store detective as they tried to leave by the swing doors. Stella watched on in shame and horror as they were taken to an office and searched. From their pockets were pulled beads, necklaces and cufflinks, anything that had taken their fancy. Only some pretty fast talking from Stella and the excuse that these were disturbed children from a special school got them off. And she had to promise never to take them to that shop again.

Now they stood outside the store and Stella felt shattered. The other two were looking slightly anxious, too.

'I'm worried,' said the leader. 'I have charge of the pills. Soon my brother will find it difficult to remain solid.'

Just as he spoke, Stella noticed that there was some commotion down the road. People were looking up and pointing at an object on the top of a building 'Something's happening,' she cried, and they walked hurriedly down the road to have a look. Then she could see what the fuss was about. High up, on the rooftop, was perched a small figure in a mini-skirt, red woollen jumper and tartan tammy.

'It's our brother!' said the leader. 'He's taken off in the wind, so he must have run out of pills. Oh dear, this will be difficult. I can will him down by mind control but we must get close enough to catch him in case he floats away.'

Stella ran back to get the car which she drove as close as she could to the building her little charge was clinging on to. Some people seemed to be putting up a ladder to reach him. Stella could see the other two holding hands and staring up at the sun. Suddenly their brother left his perch and began to float down like a balloon. The crowd gasped as he floated on over their heads towards the two little blond-haired children standing on the pavement. As he passed over them, the brothers grabbed his legs and pulled him down towards them. Stella pushed her foot down hard on the accelerator, stopped as they quickly bundled themselves into the back, and drove off fast, not stopping until she was on the other side of town.

Once the wayward brother had had his dose of pills, he was in good condition again and able to recount his adventures to the others. It seems that he had been befriended by a nice young man who took him to a place where he insisted on him drinking some fizzy stuff from a bottle. He had then wrestled with him and torn off those nice frilly knickers. Offended by the violence, the brother had quickly left in a huff, but then he had found himself so full of gas that he could not stop himself floating up to the rooftops.

Hearing all this, Stella began to laugh until tears ran down her face. 'Oh dear,' she gasped, 'there must be an easier way to help you than this.'

The travellers did not laugh with her. In fact, they were dead serious. 'From what I have seen of your planet, Stella, I do not like it much. There is dirt and noise and much confusion.'

'You could be right; perhaps I had better return you to your spacecraft,' she said. 'But there is something I wanted you to see, something I thought you could take part in. It's related to your mission and might give you some insight into the sort of problems we have to face here on Earth.'

'It sounds interesting,' agreed the leader. 'And if you think it will help us, then I think we should go.'

'Good, let's chance it,' said Stella. 'And it will give Trevor a shock to see me even before he meets what I've brought with me,' she muttered to herself.

'I'm going to take you to what's called a television studio,' she explained. 'I want no more nonsense; stick with me, sit still and say nothing. Is that clear?'

'Perfectly,' they said in unision.

Stella realized that she was feeling quite anxious about meeting Trevor again. After all, she had deserted him rather suddenly and given little explanation for her behaviour. She wondered if he would be pleased to see her or whether he was still angry at her for the way she had treated him.

Stella still held a pass for Trevor Bevan's popular evening TV show. She smiled as she thought of his quick sarcastic humour which always made his live show go down so well. Tonight, as she knew from the newspaper, there was to be one of those lively discussions in which a group of progressive working-class women challenged a group of intellectuals on their assumptions.

'It ought to be of great interest to you,' Stella informed her little companions, 'because the subject is the population explosion.' They walked down the windowless corridors which seemed like a rabbit warren.

'The air of your planet is quite foul,' the leader replied, 'but we fail to see that the place is over-populated.'

They entered the brightly lit, stuffy television studio and Stella led them to a row of seats. Other people in the audience pushed past them and jostled for seats. 'Never mind. Sit, listen and learn,' Stella advised. 'After the programme I'll introduce you to my friend Trevor.'

Just as she spoke, Trevor walked into the studio. He was accompanied by a thin, nervy man on one side and a slim blonde-haired girl on the other.

He saw Stella immediately. 'Great Scott! Stella, where have you sprung from?'

Stella thought he looked distinctly shocked at seeing her and not at all delighted, as she had secretly hoped he would be. 'I've come up from the country,' she explained. 'I thought my friends would enjoy your show.'

Trevor stared at her strange companions with a look of puzzlement on his handsome face. He seemed to be about to say something else when he was interrupted by the blonde girl at his side.

'Come on, darling,' she said urgently. 'We have four minutes . . .'

Not once did this girl look at Stella but Stella's observant eye did not miss the sparkling ring on her third finger. It was the same ring that Stella had returned to Trevor last year.

'Was that your man?' enquired the leader, as Trevor and his companions walked away.

'Used to be,' Stella replied shortly.

'He does not like us,' the traveller announced.

'That's because he doesn't know you,' Stella replied.

'That's not a reason,' said the traveller. 'And if he's typical of your great men, then I'm very disappointed.'

Stella sniffed. 'Oh, don't be misled. Trevor is not a great man, but he is very useful. If you came to my teaching hospital, you would meet clever, dedicated men there.'

'I trust what you say, Stella,' he said. 'But I dislike him because I can tell that he has hurt you.'

Stella looked down gratefully at her tiny loyal friend, whose keen blue eyes missed little. 'Well, it wasn't all one-sided,' she murmured, 'but thank you anyway.'

Once installed in the front-row seats, Stella turned around to look at the rest of the audience. 'We could be in for a lively evening,' she said.

From the start the debate went into vigorous action. Stella's little companions were clearly terrified of the bright studio lights and recording equipment. They cringed and huddled up together, but they watched very intently as the panel of pundits and experts seated themselves in front of Trevor up on the stage.

The cameras were rolling. Immediately Trevor switched into his performance mode. 'We are here,' he said to the camera, 'to discuss the population growth. We have a mixed audience here today who are eager to throw questions at our distinguished panel of experts.'

Stella looked carefully at this panel. There was Dr Enid Strang with her thin scraggy neck, staring haughtily down at the studio audience. Professor John Samson was scratching his bald pate and yawning, but the other two – a middle-aged novelist of some repute and a bright young Justice of the Peace – looked alert and ready for anything.

Dr Strang started the debate with a short, well-informed speech. This she delivered in a monotone that was not quite soporific. 'So something must be done about the population explosion,' declared Dr Strang as she wound up her speech, 'or by the end of the century it will be impossible for our planet to survive.'

'Well, they had better put down a few of the oldies,' cried a wit from the back row. There was a lot of laughter.

But Dr Strang was not amused. In fact, she looked very annoyed. 'We are here to discuss the birth-rate problem,' she snapped. 'It would be helpful if the humorous person could keep his comments to himself.'

There was another titter of amusement and the same wit cried, 'You might be one of the first, Enid; you've had a good innings.'

At this difficult moment, Trevor interrupted, changing the trend of the argument with professional agility. 'How many children have you, madam?' he asked, pointing to a sturdy woman sitting just behind Stella.

'Four,' she replied truculently, 'and I wouldn't mind if I had six.'

Trevor stirred matters up. 'But I understand that your husband has been unemployed for the past year.'

The woman scowled. 'So what? We love our

children just as much whether we got money or not. And we look after them proper.'

'Do you?' said the Justice of the Peace, a portly man with a very smug expression on his face. 'I suspect that the state does that for you.'

This remark was like a red rag to a bull. Voices called from all sides: 'That's unfair . . .' 'No call for such comment . . .' The woman was red-faced by now. She stood up waving a big fist. 'What do you know, you git? Ain't wanting for a penny all your life, I bet.'

'That's beside the point and entirely irrelevant,' interjected the dogmatic Dr Strang. 'If you want to have a big family, you should consider why. Family size is no longer a private decision. It is one that affects the whole of society and we must learn to be responsible about it.'

'Oh nuts!' declared the irate woman, now almost in tears.

'Tell me, madam,' said Trevor pointing to a woman in the middle, 'do you think birth control should be a matter for the state to control?'

The woman spluttered. 'No, I do not! No prime minister is going to tell me how many kids I can have!'

The laughter and argument were uproarious. Trevor was looking distinctly worried as the debate came close to getting out of hand.

Jumping in to quieten the audience again, Trevor then invited Professor Samson to talk about how he would see signs that the end of the world was in sight. The professor did not give an uplifting speech (his subject did not help) but it certainly had the effect of restoring order.

Everyone was bored. Even Stella tried desperately not to yawn. Her companions had been listening very intently but she could tell that even their minds were beginning to wander, and the one in the mini skirt was sitting in an obscene pose, his skirt up, his legs apart and what remained of his frilly knickers exposed. There were whispers and giggles from the young women behind, who had got hold of the torn lace of the knickers and were pulling it so that the knickers were slowly unravelling. Their suppressed giggles grew louder.

The old professor hesitated and looked puzzled. He had not meant his lecture to be funny. Trevor, now white with temper, looked angrily in Stella's direction. What was going on? It was those damned kids with Stella who seemed to be causing the disturbance. But with the cameras rolling on a live show, there was nothing he could do except use his skill as a presenter. He would have to wait for the break.

Valiantly, Trevor managed to stop the dreary old professor. Where *did* the researcher find him? Someone will be sorry, he vowed.

'And now it's time to take a break,' Trevor almost snarled into the camera. 'We'll be back in a couple of minutes.' He glared furiously at Stella and her peculiar companions. Then something inside him snapped. It was all *their* fault that the show was going wrong that evening, and he knew what he was going to do about that . . .

Stella was just talking quietly to the leader about television, when two burly men approached.

'Excuse me, madam,' said one, 'but the young people with you must leave. I've instructions to escort them out.'

Stella looked up in puzzlement, but the brothers, sensing danger, suddenly panicked. One of them darted from his seat and ran between the legs of one of the commissionaires and tripped him up. The man fell heavily on top of his companion who seemed to get the idea that resistance was being offered. In no time at all a skirmish was in progress in the studio.

Ten minutes later, having held up Trevor's live show for a good five minutes, Stella and her three companions were ejected through the studio door. Telling the commissionaires what she thought of them, she marched to her car, and she and the little men from Moonecticus climbed in.

She put her foot down hard and did not stop until they were out of London. The little men were very quiet sitting there on the back seat. In the rearview mirror, she thought they looked sorrowful. All that violence had probably upset them, she thought.

Turning to look at them, she saw that one of them was propped up between the others. 'What's the matter?' she asked.

'My brother is hurt,' said the leader.

Stella immediately pulled over and stopped the car. 'Why didn't you tell me? Wait a minute, my bag is in the boot.' Staring at the ailing little man, she saw that the tiny arm just above the elbow was quite flat and a sticky white fluid oozed from it.

'Oh dear,' she said. 'He must have crushed his arm.

I'll bind it up. It's strange how your blood is colourless and that your brother made no sound to indicate that he was hurt.'

The leader stared at her. He seemed to have a distant look on his face. 'I request that you drive home quickly,' he said. 'I have a medical kit in the spacecraft. Your drugs will be of no use to him.'

Stella was prepared to do as he said. She started the car again and drove speedily home. When they got there, Stella and two of the aliens carried the third into the barn. They insisted that they care for their brother in their own manner.

Stella paced up and down outside the barn feeling very frustrated. It was her natural instinct as a doctor to want to take over the treatment and help but she was impotent in this situation. Was he going to die? She raged against her uselessness. She could hardly bear it.

The leader soon assured Stella that his brother was not going to die. 'He will not die but we must put him to rest. We are afraid of unknown microbes that might invade once our skin has been broken. Unfortunately, to help him it will be necessary to use up our entire supply of drugs. This means that we shall have to leave your planet unexplored and return home.'

With her hands stuffed into the pockets of her old windcheater, Stella walked on the beach alone. As she walked she turned over in her mind the disastrous events of their visit to London. It was all her fault that these things had happened. She should never have been so stupid as to take the little creatures to the studio. What an idiot she was. She hadn't done it to help her visitors. No, she had done it merely to satisfy a selfish desire to see Trevor again. As a result of that selfishness, one of her new friends was very ill and all three of them were being forced to leave sooner than they might. Despair tugged at her heart.

She came off the beach and walked down a winding lane edged with hawthorns and trailing blackberry bushes. She loved it here in this still, quiet world where only the birds disturbed the stillness. She took a deep breath of the salty sea air. It did little to clear the confusion that filled her head.

Suddenly, from the barn she heard a strange high-pitched sound. Walking down the lane, she hesitated to look in at the spacecraft which seemed to have assumed a peculiar kind of radiance. From the entrance, the leader appeared, clad once more in his sheath-like suit. 'Come in, Stella, welcome aboard our ship.'

As if in a trance, Stella stepped on to the platform, then into the circular structure of the ship. Inside it was very light, and warm brilliance pervaded the air.

It was quite large inside the ship. Most things were circular, and in many ways it was very much like a balloon.

In a small cot by the wall lay the wounded little man, more like a fish again as he was once again dressed in his silvery suit. His arm was on a frame and bound up with the same skin-like material.

The third brother was sitting before a panel of instruments which emitted the high-pitched sounds.

'My brother is sleeping and cannot converse,' the

leader informed Stella. 'But we have successfully repaired the damage to his arm.'

Stella sat down in the circular cubicle next to the sick alien. As she sat there, she felt her tiredness and depression leave her. A rich glowing feeling came from within, as if she had just come in from a glorious bathe in the sun.

'We are leaving soon, Stella,' said the leader. 'It is a pity we were not able to complete our mission.' He looked very sad.

'I will be sorry to lose you,' Stella replied quietly. 'Perhaps some day you will return.'

'Not in our lifetime,' the leader replied. 'It was a very hazardous and expensive journey, and we are not home yet. I have to say that we were very disappointed in your capital city. Such grief, quarrels and resentment are spiritually exhausting.'

Stella sighed. 'It's not all like that, it's a big world. Perhaps I did not go the right way about it. I wanted to protect you,' she explained.

'But Stella, what excuse is there for those screaming argumentative females and aggressive young men?' the leader asked.

'It was a debate and I suppose many people felt strongly about the idea of their childbearing being controlled in any way,' she explained lamely.

The leader sniffed. 'Population explosion! I have seen many, many uninhabited places on your planet. Nowhere is it like that on Moonecticus any more.'

'It's hard to visualize a place so overcrowded,' Stella answered.

'Maybe, but we are happy,' explained the leader. 'We get on, we co-operate, and we live for the welfare of each other,' he added proudly.

'I believe you,' Stella said quietly. 'It's impressive.' Her brown eyes regarded him seriously.

The alien's gentle hand stroked her arm. 'I shall miss you, my lovely Earth woman. And I shall take your memory for ever in my heart.'

Tears welled up and Stella said chokingly, 'I've grown awfully fond of you. In a way I wish I were going with you.'

'There is little reason for you to stay here,' said the leader. 'It is very possible that on Moonecticus you will fully regain your health and live a good long life.'

'Oh please, don't torment me,' Stella cried. 'It would be impossible for me to live in your atmosphere.'

'But I told you,' said the leader, 'many centuries ago, Earth men landed on our planet. They lived and died there. My brothers and I are descended from them – our hair is a living reminder. The rest of our people are completely hairless and our kind are very rare,' he explained.

Stella nodded. 'I do so want to believe you,' she said.

'You are an intelligent educated woman, and I would not mislead you,' the leader told her gravely. 'I would be most happy to introduce you to our world.'

Confused thoughts rushed through Stella's mind. She struggled hard to think clearly but the warm hand spreading radiance through her made her feel almost too good, a strange excitement soared in her. Hell or heaven. Moonecticus could be either, but why should she care? The visitors had given her back her health and now she could repay them. And besides, as a scientist, she was being offered the most amazing opportunity imaginable.

Now her mind was working hard. 'If I can come with you, perhaps my knowledge of a new drug will benefit your population. It is a pill which prevents women from breeding too often. If we adapt it, it might even control your population. Then, who knows? By the sound of it, yours might end up being a better world than mine.'

'We would be delighted and most honoured, Stella, if you came with us,' said the leader. 'And if you can introduce this drug to our population as you describe, then our mission will not have been a failure after all.

'We will leave at nightfall. You may bring books and some food but not much else. My brother will quickly make you a suit to protect you from the radiation we must travel through. You will love our clean, sweet air, and slowly your body will acclimatize itself to our atmosphere. I have to say that this place is foul, it smells of dirt and disease. I for one shall be very happy to return home.'

He smiled a radiant smile at Stella, and she returned it.

When dusk descended over the coast a strange whining sound was heard behind the copse. All over the country there were reports of people seeing a flying saucer. It made the evening news but the excitement died down when no one could produce hard evidence that such a thing had existed.

So Stella, warm and tranquil in a silvery skin suit, and yet excited at the prospect of her new life ahead, left her planet behind. She felt she had not one care left in the world as she headed towards the new one.

One week later, an article in a national newspaper caught the eyes of a certain television presenter. The headline read: 'FAMOUS LADY DOCTOR DISAPPEARS: SUICIDE SUSPECTED'. The article went on to describe how Dr Stella Howard's cottage on the marsh had been found deserted, and a note had been pinned to the door announcing that all her effects were to be sold and the money given to Cancer Research. No trace of her body had yet been found, but suicide was suspected as it was known that Dr Howard had suffered from terminal cancer and had become a recluse in the past few months.

Trevor Bevan was to wonder about the last time he had seen Stella during that television debate on his show. How odd that she had turned up so unexpectedly like that, accompanied by those odd-looking and very badly behaved children. Who *were* they, for heaven's sake? And he was to remain forever guilty about having Stella and her friends thrown out of the studio. But not so guilty that he wasn't soon putting his mind to his next important television discussion: 'Can there be life on other planets?'

When Kelly Came Home

When I look at my lovely daughter Kelly sunbathing in our garden, my thoughts drift back to when I was her age. How different I was at fourteen! It still amazes me that this tall slim creature in a yellow bikini is my child, my daughter. The contrast is so striking now. When I was a young teenager, I was long and lanky, even gawky, with horrible thin, mousy hair and big goofy teeth. In spite of my gawkiness, my main qualities as a child were an athleticism and ease with my body which made me good at school games. I excelled at swimming, netball and running, and this made me very popular with my schoolfriends.

I had one particular friend who was, physically, completely different to me. Wilma was a tiny, blonde girl, whose hair was a pretty dusty-ash colour. It was always neatly trimmed with a silky fringe cut straight, above sky-blue eyes, edged with dark lashes.

Wilma and I became friends during our penultimate year at school. We shared a sense of humour and a practical attitude towards life. We were about as clever as each other – which wasn't saying much – and we had no sense of rivalry to tear us apart. We were the perfect duo. We became inseparable and my big family of brothers, and even my parents, were prompted to make humorous remarks about our different appearances – like chalk and cheese, they all said – and how my conversation became obsessively peppered with references to Wilma.

Wilma and I would stroll home from school together each day. We would be arm-in-arm, tiny blonde Wilma and long lanky Lou. I always had a grin from ear to ear, and always seemed to be laughing. But what there was to laugh at, I was never quite sure.

We would say goodbye at the street corner, and Wilma would set off for her part of the town with its old working-class cottages, while I would head for our more prosperous area with its modern detached bungalows. In spite of all my efforts and begging, I could never persuade Wilma to come home to my house.

'Oh, please, Wilma,' I would plead. Do come and have some tea.'

But every time she would refuse. 'No thanks, Lou,' she said. 'My mother will be waiting for me.'

Around her neck on a string Wilma always wore a latch key. This adornment greatly added to my admiration of Wilma. After all, no one ever trusted *me* with a latch key.

Wilma never once invited me to her own house and she did not tell me about her family either.

Because I knew so little about her home life, I began to imagine what it was like. I surrounded Wilma with mystery and intrigue. In my fantasies, she became all sorts of things – a changeling, a princess in disguise, a fairy queen. Even in those far-off days I had an excess of romantic imagination.

One Saturday afternoon my dreams were somewhat brought down to earth. I had been taken to the cinema by my two elder brothers. After the film I lolled by the ice-cream stand while my brothers deserted me for a glass of beer in the pub. As I stood there, I suddenly saw Wilma coming down the high street pushing a heavy wheelchair in which sat a wizened old lady.

I yelled: 'Wilma!' as loudly as I could but my friend seemed too preoccupied to notice me. I did not dare dash across the road, as was my first impulse, because I knew I'd get a mouthful from my brothers, so I hurried to the zebra crossing. But by the time I had crossed the road, Wilma had made off quickly down a side street. Oddly enough, I felt that she was avoiding me and that annoyed me.

On Monday, during school break, I went up to Wilma. 'Stuck up thing, Wilma,' I said crossly. 'I saw you in town and called out to you but you ignored me.'

Wilma's fair skin blushed scarlet. 'I was with my mother,' she said quickly.

I frowned at her. 'What, that old lady?' I immediately regretted my tactless ejaculation as I watched the tears cloud Wilma's pretty blue eyes. 'My mother is a permanent invalid,' she said quietly, 'and I am the only one she has to care for her.' Her lower lip quivered slightly as she spoke.

Immediately, I was contrite.

'Sorry, love,' I muttered. 'Why don't you let me help

you?' The tears had gone and Wilma's composure had returned. 'No thanks,' she said coldly. 'I can manage.'

The last year of school arrived at last. I began to take an interest in popular music and often went out in the evenings to the local hops. Wilma never joined me. 'Don't be silly, Lou,' she would say whenever I asked her to come. 'You know I can't get out nights.'

And I felt guilty for being able to be carefree and do what I liked when my friend was burdened with such responsibilities. Not surprisingly, we began to drift apart.

On leaving school, I went to work in an office in the City. Although I still lived at home, I travelled to work by train each day, and spent very little time in my old haunts. I never saw Wilma during this time and I did not know what she was doing.

The following spring I emigrated with my entire family to Australia. Sadly, in spite of our hopes and aspirations, the immigrant life proved to be far from enjoying the land of milk and honey we had believed it to be. Everyone had a hard time. Gradually all my brothers left for the outback or the deep sea, leaving me alone with my parents in a small mill town. My father and I worked at a British-owned paper mill, while my unhappy mother stayed at home and pined for England. We were lonely, isolated and poor. Why, we kept asking ourselves, did we ever leave behind what we had and enjoyed?

But throughout this difficult period, my spirits remained cheerful if I kept good memories in my head.

And these were nearly always regarding the happy times I had with my old friend Wilma.

After two years my mother got so homesick that my parents decided to return to England. Originally I was to have gone with them, but by then I had met Paul. Paul was a shipmate of one of my sailor brothers, and I met him when he came home to supper one night. We were all greatly entertained by my brother Jim and Paul as they recalled the good and the bad times aboard their ship the HMS *Kelly*.

I listened to their banter, transfixed by the sight of this smiling blond giant sitting across the table from me. I watched those white teeth flash a wide smile and noticed how his fair curls snuggled close to the back of his clean pink neck. Although I did not say a word that first night, it was then that I made up my mind that Paul was going to be mine. He never stood a dog's chance of escaping me. I was just eighteen when we married. And it was with my parents' blessing on the day before they sailed for home.

So there we were, newly-wed in a relatively new country but with no regrets; we were tremendously happy. Paul proved himself to be the dearest and best of husbands. We moved into a small bungalow supplied by the paper mill. I still had my job there and Paul joined as a trainee engineer. We worked hard, played hard, danced, swam and played tennis and entertained in our new home. Life in the new country began to seem easier, even idyllic at times.

The following summer I became pregnant. It was terribly hot, and the creek from where we obtained our water supply was almost dry. I was instructed by the doctor to boil every drop of water we used. Coming from a land where there is a plentiful supply of fresh water, I had a tendency to be careless of such warnings.

Repeatedly Paul warned me not to drink from the tap.

'Oh, don't fuss,' I always replied.

Paul was particularly concerned for my health now that I was pregnant. He was looking forward to being a father. At times he could barely contain his excitement. 'It's going to be a girl,' he would say. 'A sweet little girl and we will call her Kelly.'

'What, after a ship?' I cried. 'I'll see we don't!' And he would hug me tight and stroke my growing belly.

So we argued, laughed and joked, as was our way. Wallowing in our happiness, I then did a very thoughtless, stupid thing. After working hard in the garden in the heat of the sun, I went in and drank a cup of unboiled water straight from the tap. The result of this was a fever that proved to be typhoid. I was a long time recovering and during that time I lost my lovely little baby girl.

'We have plenty of time to have more children,' my loving husband consoled me. But it was not to be. The surgeon informed me that a post-natal infection made it unlikely that I would ever conceive again. He said I must get used to the idea of a life without children.

I was heartbroken and deeply depressed. I felt utterly helpless and that I had let my fine husband down. My health began to deteriorate. Lanky, laughing Lou became thin, scraggy and irritable. Paul became extremely worried and decided to save up and send me home to England for a long holiday. Sadly, I had to go alone. 'I cannot come with you, Lou,' he said. 'I must finish my training. But once I pass my exams I'll come over and bring you home. Then we will travel back together. It will be like a second honeymoon, darling.'

I pulled a long face, but gently he persuaded me. 'It will do you so much good to see your parents and your old home again,' he encouraged.

My parents welcomed me with open arms. Their love and attention did much to restore my mental health. I missed Paul dreadfully, but soon settled back in that old familiar environment. Friday was still market day and I trotted along as always to the flea market, to browse among the rows and rows of stalls selling second-hand gear, old clothes, tools, Victorian bric-à-brac. I just loved the atmosphere, it was part of me – the crowds, the bustle, the shouting stallholders. I remembered how I used to come down here with Wilma during our lunch break and we would wander arm-in-arm down the street, pushing and shoving as much as we were pushed and shoved. One Friday a few weeks after I had come home, I was sitting outside a café drinking a cup of tea and taking in the lively scenes around me. As I sat there, a small toddler climbed up on the chair beside me. I stared at her. There was something oddly familiar about those sky-blue eyes that gazed up at me in a melancholy wonder. I smiled at the child in a friendly way and she scampered off. As I watched her go, I was amazed to see Wilma come into my line of vision. She was by one of the stalls. There was the same neat head, the white face and blue eyes. In a flash I realized that the child had reminded me of Wilma. How very extraordinary, that she should then appear before me!

'Hallo, darling,' I cried. 'Is it really you?'

Wilma stared at me, and then said, 'Hallo, Lou, long time no see.' She smiled shyly, I thought.

'I've been in Australia,' I explained. 'Come and sit down. Let me buy you a cup of tea . . .'

Wilma hesitated and looked over her shoulder. At that moment, the little toddler came bounding back. Wilma frowned. 'I told you to stay put,' she said crossly, pulling the child roughly by the arm.

I put out a protective hand and the little one snuggled close to me. 'Is she yours, Wilma?' I asked. 'She's darling. What's her name?'

'Kelly,' Wilma replied abruptly. She picked up a suitcase and began ramming the rubbish from a small temporary stall into it. I felt rather distant as a wave of memories swept over me. Kelly, the child is called Kelly. My own little girl would have been called Kelly if she had not died. Tears pricked my eyes and I swallowed hard to hold them back.

'I'm packing it up now,' said Wilma. 'There's nothing doing today.' Her tone of voice was hard and common, something I had never noticed before.

We set off together. I held the little girl by the hand as Wilma plodded along carrying the heavy shabby suitcase by her side.

'I'm pleased that you're also married,' I chatted pleasantly, my spirits returned.

'I'm not,' Wilma answered abruptly. 'Got her on a night out. I've never seen him since.'

Well, I did not disguise my feelings of shock. That such a thing should happen to gentle little Wilma! I did not know what to say so we walked on in complete silence, with Kelly's warm hand in mine and Wilma morose and quite uncommunicative until we eventually reached the dreary tenement that was now their home.

'Lower yourself and come in if you wish,' said Wilma with obvious bitterness. It was a direct challenge which I was prepared to meet. So up those dirty stairs I went to that tiny bed-sit.

In the small untidy room I washed Kelly and put her to bed. Wilma lolled in an old chair smoking long black cigarettes.

'How is your mother?' I asked blithely, trying to make conversation.

'She's dead,' she said crisply.

'I'm sorry,' I replied.

'No need,' returned Wilma. 'She suffered hell. And then me getting into trouble finished her off.' She gave a sardonic grin. 'First time I ever got let out I fell for that kid. A right mug, wasn't I?'

I did not know how to answer, I was so embarrassed.

'Went on holiday,' Wilma continued. 'A social worker took care of mother for a week . . .'

'Oh, please, Wilma,' I interrupted her. 'No regrets. Your little girl is lovely, you are a very lucky woman.'

'Oh, it's all right for the likes of you to preach,' Wilma snapped at me viciously. 'I have got no freedom,' she complained. 'I can't get a regular job, I can't even get a night off. That bloody kid holds me down all the time.'

I did suddenly feel slightly ashamed of my thoughtlessness. Yes, life must be extra hard for her having no one to help her out in any way. But I knew what to do. 'I'll babysit for you,' I volunteered.

Wilma's expression brightened. 'Will you?' she said eagerly. 'Can you come tomorrow?'

I agreed. 'Of course,' I said. 'I should love to.'

After that, for many evenings I sat in Wilma's grim untidy room and babysat for little Kelly. How I loved, fussed and cared for that unwanted child! I tucked her up in bed and told her stories straight out of my head – about magic lands and fairies, princes and princesses. And after the child had fallen asleep, a comforting thumb in her mouth, I would sit and wait for the return of her errant parent who came home later every time, sometimes drunk and very dishevelled.

One night Wilma came back so late that I missed the last bus to my own home. I sat in the taxi back telling myself that I was a chump, and that would be the very last time I babysat for irresponsible and thoughtless Wilma.

For a week or so I kept to my resolution. I did not go near the house or the market, but even so, I kept imagining Kelly's soft warm hands in mine, or her plaintive expression and pink, tear-stained cheeks.

One Saturday afternoon, I saw Wilma in the street

when I was in town shopping with my mother. She was looking very strained. Her nice blonde hair was lank and greasy, and her face was blotchy as if she had been crying. Kelly was in a shabby old pushchair and wore a shabby yellow cotton dress. Her tiny nose was red and runny, and her sky-blue eyes looked reproachfully up at me.

My mother was appalled. 'Why, is that nice little Wilma? And it doesn't look as if she takes much care of that child.'

The pitiful sight of the two of them got to me. The next day, Sunday, I set out for that dreary dwelling once more. Wilma was still in bed. Kelly was out of bed but not dressed. Wearing stained pyjamas she played on those filthy stairs. I handed Wilma a cold flannel for her face and made her a cup of hot sweet tea. All the while a voice in my head kept saying: 'This is no business of yours.' I washed and dressed Kelly and gave her some cornflakes in a chipped bowl, the only receptacle I could find.

Wilma was rather sulky but the reason for that was soon clear: 'Phew, what a hangover!' she complained. 'I had so much on my mind that I drank a whole big bottle of wine last night,' she said without any sign of remorse or guilt.

'For pete's sake, why?' I demanded.

'Well, I've got the chance of a good job,' Wilma replied. 'I was worried because I think I shall have to turn it down.' She stopped speaking and looked intently at me for a moment, as if assessing my reaction. Then she asked what I had unconsciously been hoping she would ask: 'Would you take Kelly to stay with you for a while? Until I get settled in this job? If I can start earning a decent bit of money, I could pick myself up and get a nice place to live. You could really give me this opportunity if you would take Kelly off my hands for a week or so.'

I, of course, agreed immediately. Nothing could appeal to me more than having sole care of this young child, even for just a week. So Kelly came to my parents' house with me. She was an absolute delight and we had such great fun together. She was a very happy child. Once she was warm and well fed and stimulated, she developed marvellously. I grew passionately fond of her. We romped in the park, went to the children's library, snuggled up at bedtime, and laughed and laughed and laughed. Even my parents became attached to her during this time.

The one week turned into two weeks, which turned into three. Not once did Wilma come to visit her child. I was secretly delighted and would have been happy if we had never seen or heard from her again. But I knew that Kelly was not mine and she was the responsibility of her mother. At my own mother's suggestion, I finally went along to Wilma's lodgings, only to be told by another resident that she had 'gorn orf to Jersey' to work in a holiday camp. The news was wonderful. My mother was very annoyed and shocked that Wilma could abandon her child like that, but I was utterly thrilled.

I threw myself into the role of Kelly's mother. How I loved that child! I petted her and fussed her and bought her pretty dresses. In my heart she replaced my daughter, my own lost child. But the future was uncertain. Where was Wilma? Would she return? And besides, after Christmas my husband would arrive from Australia to join me for a short holiday before we both returned to Australia. I just did not know what would happen. As the days ticked by and I grew increasingly attached to Kelly, I wanted to write and tell Paul about this little girl. But for some reason I could never find the courage to mention her in my letters. Perhaps I was afraid that he would not want his own dead child replaced by a stranger or maybe I was afraid that he would feel usurped in my affections. Anyway, I just hung on, hoping desperately that he would in fact share my feelings.

My parents were not at all happy with the state of affairs. They were appalled that we had not heard anything from Wilma.

'Look here, Lou,' growled my father, 'take that kid to the Welfare, otherwise you will have her on your hands permanently.'

'Perhaps, I don't mind,' I replied stubbornly.

'You'd better not get in too deep,' warned my mother. 'Husbands can be very funny about that sort of thing.'

'The mother's no good, and God knows who its father is,' grumbled my father.

'Oh, how can you be so unkind,' I wept. It didn't matter who her parents were. Kelly was perfect and I would make sure she stayed that way.

In early January Paul arrived from Australia. He

was handsome, sun-tanned and self-assured, and I was pleased to know that I was still mad about him.

However, he was very non-commital about Kelly and I often felt that I was right to think he was a little jealous of my affection for the child.

'It's a ridiculous situation,' he said one day. 'That child's mother could walk in at any time and snatch her back. Then it would break your heart.'

'Oh, no, I'm quite sure that she doesn't want her,' I insisted.

He found it hard to believe that I had not named the child Kelly myself. I could tell that he thought my involvement with her very unhealthy. 'When we get home, we will apply to adopt a newborn baby,' he said firmly. 'It will seem more like our own.'

But I was opposed to this idea. I could not face the thought of ever parting from Kelly. I put up all sorts of yarns about not wanting to return to Australia, when I knew in the back of my mind that I simply did not want to part from Kelly. Seeing that he was getting nowhere, Paul sulked, went out and got drunk. For the first time in our marriage an icy coldness existed between us.

Then one day, out of the blue, I got a letter from Wilma. It was written from a ward in a London hospital, and she was asking me to visit her.

I went there straight away, full of foreboding and very sad at the prospect of returning Kelly to her mother now she had resurfaced. But I was to have such a shock. I will never forget the sight of Wilma lying in that narrow hospital bed. She looked like a wizened old lady. I knew immediately that there was something seriously wrong and I could hardly bear to look at her.

'Hallo,' I said, as cheerfully as I could. 'Where have you been?'

'How's Kelly?' Wilma asked. Her voice was soft and weak.

'She's fine,' I said. 'She misses you,' I lied.

'I don't believe that,' Wilma said bitterly. 'She's yours if you want her.'

My heart leaped at those words but I was very confused. 'But I'm meant to be going back to Australia in a few weeks,' I said tearfully.

Wilma gazed at me coldly. 'I thought you were fond of her,' she said weakly.

'Oh I am,' I exclaimed. 'I can't bear the thought of parting from her.'

Wilma seemed to shrug her thin shoulders. 'Oh well, I suppose the Welfare will provide for her then,' she said nonchalantly.

'Oh, Wilma, she's your own flesh and blood! You can't desert her,' I begged.

'I can't help myself,' Wilma said. Her voice was flat. 'I've got my mother's complaint. It's a wasting disease and progressing rapidly. Even if I wanted to look after Kelly, I'm not going to live to have that option.' She stared at me with dull, listless eyes.

I recoiled at these words but my reply came out without hesitation: 'Don't worry over Kelly,' I choked, 'I'll always take care of her.'

Relations between Paul and me were still somewhat

strained and, when I told him the latest detail about Kelly's background, I was shocked by his response. 'Good lord, Lou,' he shouted. 'The child's mother has not only abandoned all responsibility for her, but is also a chronic invalid until she dies an early death. If her mother had it then it's possible that the girl will inherit it, too. You just don't know what you are getting into,' he warned.

I was shocked by his callous attitude. 'I can never part from Kelly,' I declared obstinately.

Paul looked furious, angrier than I had ever seen him. 'In that case, you must choose between us,' he said in a quiet, controlled voice. Turning on his heels, he stormed out of the house and went off to the pub for another binge.

I was at my wits' end. I did not know what to do. I did not want to ruin my marriage but I could not give up Kelly. At one point I had the crazy idea that my parents should foster Kelly until I had finalized arrangements for bringing her out to Australia.

My mother was not prepared to oblige. 'Don't be foolish, Lou,' she said. 'We are too old to take on the responsibility of a small child. We could not do it, and besides, it would not be allowed.'

'Let the state provide,' grumbled my father, thoroughly fed up with the situation as it stood.

Then one day a letter arrived from a social worker named Mary Walker asking me to make an appointment to see her. I did and she turned out to be young and charming. She was also sensible and informative.

'I have handled Wilma's case for some time,' Mary

told me. 'So far you are the only friend who has come forward to help her. I know you have given a temporary home to the unfortunate child, and now Wilma tells me that you wish to take Kelly for good.'

I almost wept on the social worker's shoulder. 'Oh dear,' I cried. 'What can I do? I have to return to Australia soon, and none of this can be sorted out in time. What will Kelly do?'

'Kelly will be all right in our children's home,' Mary assured me.

'But will Wilma ever recover? Will she get better?' I asked.

'There's not much chance, I'm afraid, she will slowly fade out,' she replied. 'She may go into remission for a while but she doesn't have much of a chance.'

'But Kelly, what about her?' I asked anxiously.

Mary Walker smiled. 'It's hard to tell but the tests done on Kelly have so far proved to be negative. The chances are she will be free of the disease.'

I breathed a deep sigh of relief. The social worker went on to say that Wilma had probably induced her early condition with drink and drugs. 'She has been in our care many times.'

I was shocked.

'We were anxious about the child because Wilma still drew benefit for her.'

'If I stay in this country, will it be possible for me to keep Kelly?' I asked.

'I don't see why not, as long as the parent is willing. You can foster her for a certain time and then apply for adoption. And I'll help you all I can,' Mary added kindly.

With the sight of battle in my eyes I returned home. Paul was sitting on the sofa with Kelly settled on his lap. Her fair hair was tangled with his. I felt a warm rush of feeling as I saw them; them – the two loves of my life. Overwhelmed, I dashed over and put my arms around them both. 'Oh, I do love you,' I cried.

Over the next week Paul and I seemed much closer than we had been for a while, but still we did not discuss Kelly. I spent several sleepless nights worrying about the future. I was obsessed with the idea of keeping Kelly and adopting her as my own. But I could not pluck up the courage to tell Paul of my plans. As far as he was concerned, we were returning to Australia in a week or so. In fact, I could barely bring myself to think about how I was going to solve the problem that lay ahead of me. As a result, I just shoved it aside, hoping that all would be well in the end.

I went to the hospital to say goodbye to Wilma. She looked very ill – jaundiced and extremely thin.

'I'm going into a home for incurables,' she said. 'I need my things from my bed-sit. Would you do me a favour and get them for me?'

Willingly, I went back to that shabby room, and collected all Wilma's personal belongings in a suitcase. I emptied all the papers from the drawer into an old handbag, and then took the whole lot back to the hospital.

Wilma seemed remarkably cheerful. 'I've written a letter to the Welfare,' she said. 'I've told them that I want Kelly to stay with you.'

'Wouldn't you like to see her?' I asked, amazed at

this unmaternal attitude. Wilma shook her head and pursed her lips ruefully. 'You remember me as a child, Lou, pushing my mother about in a bathchair? I would not wish such a life for Kelly.'

Tears had suddenly welled up in her eyes. To hide her emotion, she rummaged in the old handbag. 'Look,' she cried, pulling out a piece of card.

'Here's a photo of Kelly's father.' She handed me a faded snapshot. 'You can see how she got her name.'

I stared at the photograph in complete silence. I could not believe what I was looking at, and it felt as if I'd been punched in the solar plexus. Three tipsy-looking sailor boys stood outside a bar. Their arms were draped around each others' shoulders. Across their hat bands were the words: HMS *Kelly*.

'Which one?' I whispered, but I knew the answer anyway. For squinting at the camera was the face of my lovely husband. I suddenly felt very detached from reality, as though I were about to faint.

'That tall fair one in the middle.' Wilma's voice registered in my head as though in a dream.

'He's handsome,' I murmured.

Wilma smiled and nodded. 'Yes, and Kelly has his looks. I was a virgin at the time. It was my one and only time, too. Look on the back,' she urged. 'He's signed it.'

Slowly I turned over the photograph. In Paul's familiar handwriting were the words: 'To Wilma, love Paul. Pompeii, April 1956'.

I was speechless. There was really nothing that I could say. Wilma had become quite chatty as she recalled the events that led to Kelly's birth. 'I went on holiday to Hayling. It was the first time I had been with a fella, and we were both drunk.'

As she talked, I looked at her through a veil of tears.

'Keep the photo,' she said. 'You might want to show it to Kelly when she grows up.'

I left the hospital in a very confused frame of mind. Was this sudden revelation good or bad? I could not decide. On the one hand, I felt a deep resentment at the thought of Paul making love to Wilma, who had been so very attractive. But on the other hand my common sense reminded me that Paul had been single at the time, and he was just a sailor boy, with a girl in every port. I had no right to complain; he was now a kind and attentive husband to me. Somehow the situation seemed to be more clear cut and at the same time more complicated than it was before. I decided that I would keep this information to myself, at least for the time being . . .

I braced myself for the battle to keep Kelly. First I wrote to Mary Walker telling her that I had decided to stay in England and would like to foster Kelly with a view to adopting her in the future. Then, with sweet smiles, I applied my wits to Paul, suggesting that perhaps he should apply for a job in England. After all, I pointed out, now that he had qualified, he might even get a better post here, particularly since it was a British firm that had trained him.

At first Paul resisted the idea, but then he did apply for a couple of jobs and, to his astonishment and surprise, he was offered a very good position as an engineer. He was thrilled; there is nothing like success to make people sure of what they want to do.

With our plans to stay in England settled, we bought a little house quite near Paul's place of work. Kelly, now our foster child, came with us. I was blissfully happy. I had my loving husband and our beautiful daughter. Now that our plans were settled, Paul was only too happy to accept Kelly as his own daughter. She was a delightful child; her bright personality won over everyone but no one more than her dad.

After two years, we were able to adopt Kelly as our own child, six months after Wilma had died. It was very sad, but Kelly was unaware of her mother's plight and certainly never seemed to miss her.

I kept the secret of Kelly to myself. I thought it better not to stir things up by telling either Paul or Kelly the truth. But one day I came home from shopping to find Kelly perched on Paul's lap and the two of them looking at that revealing snap-shot. 'Yes,' Paul was pointing at the picture and saying, 'There's your dad when he was a sailor. Don't I look funny?'

'You look very handsome, Dad.'

As Paul looked up at me, my heart missed a beat. He must have read the message on the back of the photograph. What was he going to say? And how would I respond?

But Paul said nothing. He merely handed me the photograph and smiled broadly. 'Those were wild days,' he said quietly.

If he realized the truth, then he chose not to acknowledge it. If he did not register, then it did not matter. And in those days, before it was fashionable to tell adopted children their true origin, it was very easy for me when Kelly asked me one day if we were her real parents. I did not mention myself. 'Well,' I said with a laugh, 'just look in that mirror and tell me if you aren't the spitting image of your father.'

After that, Kelly never had any doubts that she was ours, all ours.

The Long Dream

They say a drowning man's past flashes before him when he is about to die. All I remember is this fantastic long dream . . .

I am beside a blazing fire. Looking down at my legs, I see that I am wearing a kilt and long woollen socks. Are these really my legs? They are those of a young boy . . . Indeed, they are mine. It seems that I'm a child again. My heart is thumping. I realize that I am terrified and that there is a sickening fear within me. Standing near me is a tall man with thick white hair. He is my Uncle Iain. Now I see armed men appear at the door. They rush at my uncle. I see a flashing blade momentarily suspended in the air before descending into Uncle Iain's back.

I fling myself at the attacker, hanging desperately on to his knees as he draws his sword to finish his dastardly deed. Hot blood drips on to my face. I hear my own voice screaming for mercy.

Now I am running, my feet slipping and sliding in the wet snow. All around me I hear terrible cries and curses. Women clutching children run beside me. We slither and slide up the mountain, our hair and clothes dampened by a wet, black mist.

I am crouching under a bush, its branches are white and stiff with frost. I shiver and shake and cannot keep still. Dreadful bloodcurdling screams rise up through the treacherous night air. Dear God, what is happening down there in my once peaceful home in Glencoe?

The snow falls. It builds up all around me. I am exhausted and feel very sleepy. I lose consciousness, aware of the wet mist, voices whispering, music playing . . .

When I wake up I am back on the jetty near Jeanie's Inn. I am wearing a black suit and carrying a book under my arm. There is a small cottage to the left. Jeanie is at the door. I see her lovely hair gleaming gold in the sun. She runs towards me, overwhelming me with kisses. We walk hand in hand into the old cottage, with its bright polished furniture and flowered curtains. In the centre of the room a big round table has been set for tea with a snow-white tablecloth, plates of scones and bannocks, and bowls of fresh strawberries, jugs of cream.

I remove my jacket and sit down and tuck in. It seems as if it has been a long time since I had tasted such nourishing food. Having eaten my fill, I lean back in the chair to take a good look at my lovely, much cherished twin sister.

'You look very bonny,' I remark.

'Well now, I would,' Jeanie replies with a smile, patting her high stomach to bring to my attention that she is with child. We crouch down by the fire, our bodies leaning close together, just as we used to crouch over the peat fire back home. But we are now down in

Kent, so the fire is bright with sea coal, and the iron grate shines like polished silver.

In soft Highland tones, Jeanie informs me that her husband will return home soon. 'He works on board the coasters,' she says.

'I am happy that you have found such contentment,' I say. 'But why are you so far from home?'

'I married Glenlon Campbell,' Jeanie replies breathlessly.

I gasp. 'Jeanie MacDonald! However did you get away with that?' My voice sounds shocked.

Jeanie's pretty face breaks into a smile. 'We eloped! He came round the coast on a coal barge. Oh, he's a wonderful husband, Jamie,' she cries. She hesitates and then adds, 'You know I suddenly feel safer now that you've returned, Jamie.'

I am puzzled. 'But surely there's little danger so far from home. What can you be frightened of?'

'Aunt Jess has forgiven me, that's true,' replies Jeanie, 'but great Uncle Iain has not. He may be old, but he's still very strong, and he's full of ancient clan ideas. He breathes fire and brimstone at every Campbell.'

I put my arm around her shoulders and hug her. 'Well now, then forget the Glen,' I advise her. 'You have a fine husband and are expecting a bairn. What more could you wish for?'

Jeanie shrugs and then shivers. 'I am still anxious,' she says. 'Aunt Jess has written to say that Uncle Iain has left the Glen.'

'Oh, Jeanie,' I cry, 'he's just a crazy old man. What danger is there from him?'

Jeanie pulls away and looks at me fiercely. 'It's because he's so crazy that I'm fearful for my husband and baby,' she cries. 'He takes his pipes and wanders for miles and miles.'

'Well, that may be so,' I say, 'but I doubt he will ever get as far as this place, in deepest Kent.'

The fire is burning bright. A thick mist has crept in over the sea and we can hear the boom of the breakers in the distance.

Suddenly, Jeanie leaps to her feet. 'Listen, Jamie, it's the pipes!'

I turn my ear to the door. 'Oh, 'tis only a stray gull,' I say.

'No, no, it's the wail of the piper!' Jeanie places her hands over her face. 'He's come to seek vengeance.' She cowers away from the door and starts to cry.

'Hush now,' I reassure her, 'there's nothing out there. Now go to bed. You need all the sleep you can get. I'll sit up until you're safely sleeping.'

She shakes her head. 'No, Jamie, I never rest when my husband is due. I put a lamp in the window and he signals when he begins to row ashore . . .'

I strained my ears again, and there, distantly, above the sound of the rising winds, is the unmistakable sound of a piper. So Jeanie was right. I reach for the book I am carrying. 'Come, sister, we will pray. If it is Uncle Iain, then I shall deal with him, but if it's some evil, we shall be fortified by the words of Christ.'

Jeanie seems a little calmer. I am glad to be with her at this time. 'I'll light the lamp and place it in the window,' she says. 'We'll wait for my husband and pray.'

Together we kneel in the window bay. The lamp glows brightly as the dreaded sound gets closer and closer. It seems to reach the cottage but then goes on down to the jetty.

I run to the door and pull it open. The wind rushes in, blasting me in the face. I can see an old man standing on the jetty. His long white hair is flying out in the wind. With what seems like superhuman energy, he lustily blows on the bagpipes.

'Hello, Uncle Iain,' I yell as I step towards him. The old man removes his mouth from the pipes. The music stops. He stares at me grimly, his white beard bristling. 'So, ye've come back, Parson,' he snarls at me.

'And why are you so far from the Glen?' I ask.

Uncle Iain snarls again, revealing his teeth like a wild animal. 'No place in this accursed land is far enough for me to seek my revenge,' he yells.

I see him very clearly now. He is demented, old, tired, and completely mad.

'God's curse on all the English!' he screeches. 'The bowels of our ancestors cry out for vengeance on those black-hearted Campbells! No kin of mine shall make peace with them and no kin of mine shall *live* with one!' He roars in disgust.

I send up a prayer to ask for help to calm him, and then hold out a hand to him. 'Come into the cottage,' I beg. 'Jeanie will make you welcome.'

Uncle Iain's great hand swings round and gives me a hefty push. 'I'll no enter a Campbell abode,' he hisses.

'Jeanie is with child,' I plead. 'Do not upset her.'

But far from having the desired effect, this news makes matters worse.

'A bastard, as far as I'm concerned,' he screams. 'I'll deal with its father and then I'll destroy the corruption.'

Uncle Iain begins to march back and forth, blowing wildly on his bagpipes. Rebel tunes rise up and seem to engulf me. The waves wash over the jetty as the tide rises. I walk along beside him. Glancing back at the cottage, I can see Jeanie's ripe shape in the doorway.

Back and forth we walk until my legs ache and my head feels as if it is on fire. The storm out at sea is rolling inshore. There are great crashes of thunder, flashes of blue lightning. Uncle Iain is tireless. The rain is pouring down. We are soaked to the skin. Exhausted, I finally sit down on the sea wall to watch him.

The deeper sound of a ship's siren echoes out above the sound of the pipes. Then I see just offshore someone is signalling. Glenlon Campbell is almost home.

Looking back again, I see Jeanie waving the lamp aloft to tell her man that she knew he was rowing ashore.

I feel desperate. I am a man of the cloth. I hate violence, yet I know I have to disarm the madman. All I can think of is finding some way of grabbing that long dirk, hidden in his sporran.

Uncle Iain waves the pipes aloft. 'Vengeance is mine!' he screams.

I rush forward and grab his arm. A strong hand grasps my windpipe and forces me down on my knees. Desperately I reach out, grasping the bone handle of that long sharp knife . . .

A white shape dashes past me as Jeanie runs panic-stricken towards her man. The man waves a warning arm as Jeanie, awkwardly heavy with her pregnancy, totters at the edge of the jetty.

Uncle Iain's strong bony fingers dig deep into my flesh, a mist swims before my eyes. I drag at his kilt, his strong legs, trying desperately to bring him down. Suddenly a heavy weight descends upon me. Blood flows over me. Through the night air comes a terrible cry as the waves wash over my lovely sister. I begin to fight, arms and legs thrashing wildly. I must get to Jeanie. I must save her. I push and push at the heavy weight on top of me.

Now I hear another voice through the mist. It's not Scottish but cockney. 'Take it easy, Jamie, boy,' it says. A firm hand holds me down. I open my eyes to see my sister wiping my face. My eyes are full of salt water. 'Silly fool,' says the voice of my new brother-in-law, Robert. 'First he fills himself with booze and then he falls in the briny.'

I cough and splutter, looking around in a dazed manner as I am helped back into the warm inn and the wedding reception.

When I am dry, I recall my vivid dream, my dream of a dying man. 'Jeanie, I believe I've laid your ghost,' I say.

Jeanie laughs. 'What are you talking about Jamie MacDonald? You're still a bit touched.' More seriously, she says, 'You scared us, Jamie. We thought you had drowned.'

I ignore her remark. 'Tell me,' I say, 'I know Robert's name is Campbell, but what is his full name?'

'Robert Glenlon Campbell,' she says bashfully.

I nod knowingly. Now I see what that dream is about. 'No wonder poor Uncle Iain was so agitated,' I say to my uncomprehending sister. 'He stopped you hundreds of years ago but you've gone and defied him again, and you made him angry. Old feuds never die, and neither do our spirits.'

A Little Peace and Quiet

Well, a fella has got to have a bit of peace and quiet, doesn't he? I mean, when you get to my age a guy needs it. I'm turned eighteen and that's getting on a bit in this day and age. Me ma says: 'You get up too late', while me pa says: 'You stay out too late.' What's a fella to do? I just could not stand it.

I ain't got no vices. In fact I am quite a respectable bloke in comparison to me mates. I don't drink and I don't swear, and only occasionally do I chase women. But there's one thing I do appreciate, and that's the old weed. I do like a nice quiet session with the old pot when I can afford it. Well, to cut a long story short, it was marijuana what was the cause of me moving out. I couldn't stand me ma and me pa shouting at me about the law coming down on us or me becoming an addict. It was just more than a fella can stand. So I packed my bags and went seeking peace and quiet in some lodgings of my own.

Well, I soon discovered that it's not so easy to find digs in London, especially if you are of moderate means. On one day of searching, I was given the opportunity to share with two prostitutes, four down-and-outs and a house full of people who did not speak

English. But towards the close of day, as I walked wearily around a suburb looking at the adverts, I eventually got a bit of luck. The landlady was young, blonde and pretty. She was quite obviously unused to taking in lodgers, having only recently decided to let out some rooms.

I liked the place. My room was clean and every convenience was made available. Since the room was upstairs, I felt I would be free to indulge myself as I thought fit. I was very contented. At last I had a pit of my own. This was how it should be . . . But not for long.

The next morning I was woken at the ungodly hour of eight o'clock by the sound of knocking on my door. I groaned and turned over, covering my head with a pillow.

The knocking continued. 'You there, Joe?' called a sweet voice.

'I think so,' I grunted back croakily.

'You wouldn't like to give me a push, would you Joe?' The request was still very sweetly said.

'Push yer where?' I asked, still half-dazed.

'It's my car, it won't start. I must get my boy to school and then get to the office.'

Oh dear, I thought. My landlady turns out to be one of them energetic working housewives.

'All right,' I muttered. 'I'll be out in a sec.' I put my overcoat over my pyjamas and went out into the cold early morning, something I have not done for ages.

The dog, a brown mutt, was chasing around the garden barking madly. The boy was whining and complaining about the cold while I stood in the frosty air pushing the old red banger. I was just about ready to give up when the car started with a sudden jerk. It shot forward suddenly so that I nearly fell flat on my face. The boy jumped in while his mother gave me instructions to get the dog in, and to turn off all the lights, and see that the front door was locked when I went out. So off went my pretty blonde landlady with her young son who was shooting the hell out of me with his toy gun through the back window.

I felt exhausted. I got the dog back in the house and was just moving my blue frozen feet up the stairs when the phone rang. It turned out to be an inquiry for the room, Blondy having advertised it in the local paper the previous day. It was the first of many. There was no point in going up and down the stairs. I just sat on the stairs and answered the ten or so other calls, telling them that the room was already let. Finally, I got upstairs and made myself some coffee. Even then, I realized that I was muttering 'Room's let' to myself over and over again.

Now that there was no hope of having my usual lie-in, I left the house and arrived in the office at nine instead of my normal clocking-in time of eleven o'clock. This caused much amusement among the bone-headed lot I work with. I had to put up with their mirth and pathetic wit. 'Done it in the bed, Joe?' they called, and made other disgusting remarks like that. I was beginning to wonder why I ever left home. Still, I'm not one to give up too easily. So I ignored my workmates and at the end of the day I trotted off to my new home with a bundle of fish and chips under my arm.

I settled into my room with the electric fire on. Sitting in the armchair, I ate my fish and chips and then rolled a large joint, relishing the ritual of licking the cigarette papers and sticking them together, emptying a cigarette on to them and then crumbling a generous amount of sticky black hashish on top. I rolled it up, lit it and sat back to breathe in the strong sweet smoke. I felt like swooning as the drag seemed to run along all my limbs, right down to my fingertips and toes. I realized that I had not opened the window but then I thought it did not matter. This was my room; I could do what I liked.

Suddenly, from downstairs, I heard quite a rumpus. I could hear a man's voice – no doubt Blondy's husband or boyfriend. It was loud and angry. I glanced at my door and was relieved to see that I had bolted it. I had not seen the, presumably, husband but if you can tell a man's size from his voice, then this fellow was pretty big. Not someone to tangle with.

I could hear Blondy shouting back now. This was followed by banging and doors slamming. The dog had started to bark and I could hear the boy wailing in the background. It seemed that I was the only one not to be making a racket. So much for a quiet place of my own!

Suddenly a great vibration made my records fall off their shelf. The shouting got louder and more aggressive. Finally, there was a great roar and the sound of the front door slamming. The whole house shook again. Then there was silence. Hubby must have lost the argument and retired to lick his wounds in the pub down the road.

I was standing with my ear to my door when I heard Blondy's sweet little voice call out: 'Joe, is everything all right up there? I'm sure I can smell burning.'

'No, ma'am,' I called out. 'Everything's fine.' I puffed madly at my joint to control my aggravation.

She called again: 'You sure, Joe? I can still smell something, and it's worrying me.'

I never answered. I was suddenly feeling very relaxed and I did not care any more. For a few minutes the house was blissfully quiet.

Then panic stations! I could hear Blondy yelling at the top of her voice. 'Fire! Fire!'

Now I was in a panic. I dashed downstairs, dialled the fire brigade, and then ran into the sitting room to discover dear little Blondy staring up the chimney. 'Do you think it's on fire?' she asked in a pathetic sort of way.

It was too late to stop what my 999 call had started. In no time the fire engines had descended on us. The house was invaded by fourteen large firemen just as the big husband returned from the pub to find out what was going on. Yours truly crept back to his hole. All this activity was more than my nerves could stand.

The next morning went off quite well. The previous evening, before the trouble started, I had lent Blondy my battery recharger, so her banger started like a bomb this time. Once the family had left, the house was all nice and calm. I lay in and got in my much needed rest, and arrived at the office at my usual time.

I ate my dinner in a café since I did not have any clean plates or cutlery left in my room and I had not got used to washing up yet. I got home about seven with a copy of the latest *Playboy* under my arm and the anticipation of a good smoke in my head. I was just getting settled in with my joint and my magazine when ghastly screams came up from down below. I jumped to my feet. My God, what's that?

'Help! Help!' came the cry. 'Joe! Joe! He's going to murder me.' It was, of course, Blondy.

Like a hero from the movies, I rushed out of my room and flew down the stairs to find Blondy pinned up against the front door by her beefy husband.

It appeared that she was planning to go out for the evening, dressed up to the nines. She had on full war paint, false eyelashes as well. 'I'm only having a drink with the girls,' she protested, trying to twist away from her husband's grip.

'Tell me another one,' he growled. 'Then why are you dressed up like that? Tell me that?' He gripped her tighter.

It was a domestic argument I could do very little about. I stood on the stairs like a dummy. What could I do and still stay alive?

'Help me, Joe!' pleaded Blondy again. 'He won't let me out.'

'Keep your flaming nose out of this,' the husband shouted, squeezing Blondy a bit tighter around the throat. As Blondy's face began to turn blue, I could see that I had to do something if I wasn't to witness a murder. I felt paralysed but luckily the situation was resolved by the little boy who at that moment came out of the kitchen where he had been engrossed in *Lost in Space*. Seeing what was happening to his mother, he tore up the passage, and without a word he aimed a good kick at his papa's shins. His bovver boots were small but very hard. The husband gave out a loud yell and let go of Blondy, who grabbed the boy and fled into the sitting room with a slam of the door.

Meanwhile, the husband was left hopping about the hall passage. 'Me leg, me flaming leg!' he yelled, and a lot more besides.

Well, yours truly retired once more, but I felt too emotionally disturbed to finish the joint. I actually washed up my plates and cup and saucer, trying to make as little noise as possible in case the husband picked on me too.

Later that night, the sounds of passion from the bedroom astonished me but I was relieved that the domestic battle was over. Some people are funny.

The next morning, the old banger got the blues again and refused to start. There was soppy Joe again, up with the lark cleaning spark plugs, and trotting up to the garage for a can of petrol. God knows what it had been running on for the last two miles.

Blondy gave me sweet thanks for my successful efforts. Her blue eyes glistened as she gazed into mine. I went all shivery in my shoes and glanced around quickly to see if the husband was watching. It was thrilling.

Once Blondy and little Bovver Boots had gone off for the day, I decided to take the day off. I felt quite exhausted and much in need of a bath after lying down in the road under the old banger.

I ran a nice hot bath and got in to soak in peace. I was feeling good but then a terrible thought struck me. Did I bring that confounded dog in? Seeing as it was a bitch and answered to the name of Randy, I began to worry. Just as I climbed out of the bath, I heard a great crash at the door downstairs.

'Crikey! That's the dog trying to get in.' With only a towel around me, I ran downstairs.

Standing behind the front door, I gingerly opened it. In dashed Randy followed by half a dozen other dogs as well. They all dashed into the kitchen, yapping and panting with excitement. What was I do to? I grabbed a broom and started to wave it about, shooing the dogs back down the hall and out into the garden. Five of them were cowardly creatures and turned tail at the sight of my bravery. But there was one shaggy black animal that ignored me. His pink tongue was hanging out and he kept his sights fixed on Randy, who, in my opinion, was encouraging him.

But I had a responsibility to protect Randy's virtue. I lunged at the black dog and poked him in the side. It backed away and snarled at me before slinking under the table and barking loudly. Randy ran over to the table to join him.

At that point, I decided to give up. The kitchen was freezing. I was dripping wet, dressed with only a towel around my waist. I was in grave danger of getting pneumonia. It wasn't worth it, especially if Randy wasn't going to try to help herself. I closed the kitchen door and left them to it. I went upstairs to finish my bath and then went back to bed, forgetting all about Randy and her boyfriend.

I was awakened at five o'clock by more screams. Oh, no, not another domestic upheaval, I thought. Getting up slowly to put my trousers on, I had one leg inside them when in burst my landlady, her blonde hair all over the place.

'Oh, Joe, come quick!' she screamed. 'It's Randy.'

Pulling up my trousers I went to the top of the stairs and saw Randy in the hall with her boyfriend securely attached to her back end. Back and forth they were hopping, up and down the passage. What a racket!

Little Bovver Boots was banging away at them with his gun while his beautiful mum was having hysterics in my bedroom. 'Dear me, what a situation! What'll I do?' she was screaming.

But Joe came to the fore again. I ran downstairs, grabbed a broom from the cupboard and charged like a warrior down the hall. Closing my eyes, I struck wildly several times at the copulating couple.

The canine lovers did eventually come apart but their howls and yelps were outraged. Then the male, in frustrated fury, rushed at me and tore the bottom off my trouser leg. I opened the front door quickly and the dog rushed out. Randy was left howling and crying like a baby.

I felt quite proud of my actions, but my landlady was not impressed. She had recovered from the shock and now stared at me reproachfully.

'You never had to hit them like that, Joe,' she said. 'I thought you was an animal lover.'

I stuttered my apologies. But to no avail.

'I'm changing my mind about you,' Blondy added bitterly. 'I thought you was a nice boy when you came.'

I felt ashamed and now quite rejected by my beautiful Blondy. I crawled upstairs back in my hole. Now if some kind soul with the same filthy habits as me would like to adopt me, kindly let me know. Otherwise it's back to dear old Mum. At least I can't disappoint her any more than I have already.

Yours truly,

Joe